This special signed edition of

L0$T AMЄR1CAN$

is limited to 100 copies

Jeb Burt

92

This is copy

LOST AMERICANS

PS Publishing Ltd
Grosvenor House
1 New Road
Hornsea, HU18 1PG
England

editor@pspublishing.co.uk / www.pspublishing.co.uk

To Terry and Randy

LOST AMERICANS

. . . our country will live the twenty-first century as the USSR has lived the twentieth, at war with its own imagination, having to crush its spirit in order to uphold its doctrine.
—Michael Ventura "What God on Whose Side?"

Feeding the dead is necessary.
—W. S. Graham "Implements in their Places"

A Home in the Night

AN EMPTY COOLER IN THE BACKROOM OF THE BODEGA WHERE he used the bathroom between customers called to him.

He slipped into the chest's mouth and found himself in a small, horizontal passage; behind him the square hole was bright, looking up to the hazy and distant teal of an eye. He moved cautiously and delicately onward, hunched, as if through the dark of a crowded theater; the passage expanded around him. A huge and breezy space. He shuffled in little steps, keeping his toes flat to the smooth floor, to feel for pits or obstacles; the dark seemed to pour into itself ahead of him, into a deeper place. The chest became a tiny pixel, green, and then it faded. The instant it was gone a new dot of light of the same color appeared ahead.

When he came to it he found another opening, this one set in the floor; in the light streaming up two thick, silver-scaled arms moved. At their ends: blocky, sharply razored black claws that worked the crosses of a puppeteer; silver strings descended though the opening. Above it, as if bodiless, a smooth, doughy face with vitreous eyes stared and caught the pink light in ovals. The hands moved deftly, worked the crosses. Terry kept hidden in the shadow of the pale of quartz light, terrified.

One of the arms beckoned him before he could run. The silver bracts shone like the skins of sardines. The thing smelled of oiled steel and engine burn as he came alongside it. Shifting both crosses into one hand, it took hold of Terry's shoulder and pulled him to the rim. The hand let go; Terry looked down. The promenade at dusk sat directly below; he saw two bodies by the bronzed skating rink, seated, a woman and a young man. He recognized himself, and the old lady. He was drawing her portrait while she sat proud as a queen before the court artist. Wires, which he had not noticed when he was down there, fastened to her hands, elbows, head, eyelids, feet, stomach, knees, scalp and buttocks. Watch this, the creature said, and made the woman arch her arm over her head, flamenco-like. The other Terry said something to her, and made a polite gesture for her to be still.

The thing gave Terry a villainous, amused look. Should we listen to you?

How is he—am I—?

Sighing, it set down the crosses. The woman resumed her position. I see you have no time. You are not all you, it said, is the easiest way to say it.

What am I?

You, here, are that matters.

Which is? Terry's heart pounded; he was glad, at least, that him here had a heart.

You are your Perception, I guess are the words for it, though they're not very good words. To Terry's blank stare the angel said nothing, his wide eyes encircled softly with mounded doughy lids;

the glass dark, inscrutable on the boy. He took up the puppeteer's crosses and threw them into the hole, and took Terry's shoulder again in his claw. He led the young man away into the dark.

A higher breezy space. A shell around them of faint susurrus that fades when their voices fade to murmur; it comes from all places equally, far off, a sphere of noise. The small green door is gone. The floor is a hard metal that thuds. The angel's talons click, with each raising of his knee comes a faint aspiration of hydraulics. The dark holds to Terry, kneads him, a woman wanting him to stay.

Wind. Metal squeals; noises of tempering hammer come on wind from one side of the sphere. From the other, soft, quiet, humid breath. Things are knocking under the steel; softer than the metal, the clinks are not steely. They are woody; pale knuckles rapping metal inches below his feet. Sweat runs down his thigh to the interred sound. He feels the whispers, now moans, that band in circles of drafts, minds, eels; he can almost make out their tumid flanks and beyond them, the stars. He seems to see faces peering in at the edge, or shadows. He squints; they vanish.

His eyes adjust to the dark: metal gantries rise along the walls of the sphere. A platform hangs from flanges at the apex, twisting in the wind. Before Terry is a chair of canvas like the one he left behind on the promenade. He wonders, is he to sit? They pass, the angel's great black orbs fixed glassy and dreamy into the unexplained chamber.

The dead.

Yes. But the living too. The round glass of the angel's eyes deepen from jade to saffron, with a red embryo in the center.

I don't understand, Terry says. How could you—

I'd bring them here. This place is in between; it blisters the outer skin between your world and His. His eye goes right past it. It took me nearly eternity to find; and it's taken me as long to find my way inside. I've worked hard to prepare it for them.

Terry looks at the vast warehouse of stone and star.

This is where you'd bring them?

It will be comfortable soon.

You *can* bring them—

I think so, the angel says, frankly; I've learned some tricks.

Why me, then? When you have such ability—I draw tourists. I live in a shitty studio in Queens. I'm not devout.

Terry stands, calm, under the great arch of the cavern. The air is soothing and cold on his face. He feels the stars radiating above and below; he is hidden from them in this cave but he can feel them. It is the ultimate place to hide. He feels good here. So?

The angel's grin is grateful, but tentative, guiding him along a track, but at Terry's quizzical look he quashes the smile and raises one glittering scaled arm in the direction of the cave's unending length. His scales burn, giving off their own light, and he opens his glass talons.

They begin to appear. Slowly, dim. Not quite there, they seem to rise each out of a single star through the dusted floor. Gentle light inside faces spreading back through the chamber. Eyes in faces Terry would have loved to draw, had already in his arms and long fingers to draw, stored, hopeful, their bodies and souls straggling behind their burning heads. They all stare at him, millions on millions of irises in the cave of the night, through a new enduring silence, like stone.

They're voiceless, the angel says, softly, out of consideration to them. The breath I can spare will be enough for them to remain here, with us; just enough to animate the pieces. They won't speak again.

Terry doesn't answer.

I need you to draw them, Terry.

Terry quietly stares at the endless faces that watch him, his hands cold, and his eyes hot. It isn't right, he says.

I can't give them what was theirs if I don't know what was taken. I can only see so much, the angel says, looking down. The metallic whir in his throat has become rusty, corroded with emotion.

Are you some—

I don't know, the angel says. I don't think so. I've looked all through your books; I've always been close. Talking to Him. Listening to Him sleep. I think I'm an angel.

I want to go home.

You don't have a home, the angel says. Will you do it?

Take me back, Terry says. I need time.

Time, says the angel, I have to say, is up.

We have little time, the angel says. He'll find us; He always does.

Please, Terry says.

Brace yourself, Terry.

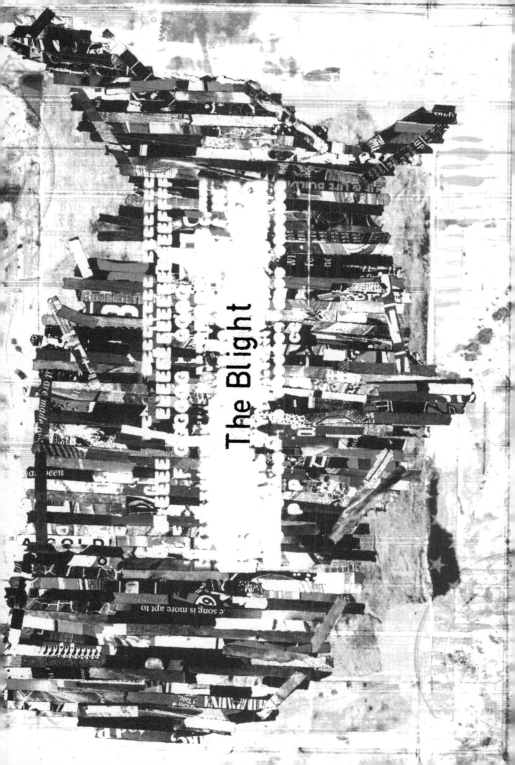

The Blight

"I will bring one more . . ."

—God, Exodus 11:1

THE PLAGUE DESCENDED SUDDENLY. IT CAUSED NO SURPRISE.

The towers downtown became polymer and styrene spires. Cars plasticized to opal propylene as their tires fused into the cement of coast routes.

The women dancing in the Jelly Julie on Sunset monstrously thermoset before the horny men, as the petrochemical bane reached the Central Valley. It hesitated at the edge of the migrant towns and great vale of farmland, as if to weigh how the urban populace met this change. When the people continued the old lifestyle, merely titillated by this novelty world of vinyl and epoxy, the polymerization surged on through cropland. The film moguls and actors and club musicians, porn titans and courtesans, drank piña coladas under acrylic palms along Malibu sands and Mulholland lawns of emerald isobutyl. The plague hardened the San Joaquin Valley to an inedible breadbasket of decorative fruit.

Famine set in. Others followed the fused strippers: Melrose sidewalks crammed with mannequins in aspect of shoppers, peering into jewelry store windows. The skin carameled in the California sun into dulce de leche, the eyes shining.

Those who could afford horses fled northeast into the Rockies, but seemed to bring the plague. At the ends of shotguns they were turned from mountain towns, the road an eel of crisp resin at their heels. At the east base of the American Cordillera, the Armed Forces erected a battery to halt the movie moguls and stars, haggard advertisement tycoons and champion surfers, whose wealth and love of good living kept them before the blight. The Rocky Mountains vulcanized under their tired feet. Their horses hardened. Ice slopes glacéd. Tors—Bakelite—reflected the sun like knives of obsidian as their clothing fused into their necks. The cursed Californians stared from ledges amid rubber pine, a long show-window of alp trekkers between seasonal shipments; they stared, doleful, across the rolling living grass of the Great Plains, from which their forbearers brought crop to the Central Valley and to which they ushered death. Slowly, bodies catalyzed and howitzers fired upon screaming mannequins wobbling down interstates.

The plastic blight ended at the Great Divide. As the nation mourned the West, agleam every sunset like a derelict candy land, the Midwest and East Coast conceded the logic of such a plague coming from California.

A gold blight hit New York. The silver hypodermic of the Empire State pushed gold into the sun. The Chrysler Tower and architecturally vervy investment banks in lower Manhattan rippled and shone. The auric creep pursued investment bankers and commodity men through Ohio. Heavy artillery eliminated them in the rolling corn.

The Blight

Southerners and plainsmen thanked Heaven for its benevolence. Two years later the black flesh was there. Remaining Americans waited. Shined eyes stared from softening skin and dimmed.

The Dogs

IN VARIOUS SIZES AND HUES THEY CAME, COATS DARKENED BY flood—small fat ones buoyant cocktail weenies, long thin ones frail-looking as estuarial birds, and great ones, biblical beasts, wood barrels strapped at their chins. My girlfriend said these were saints but I didn't see what she meant until I saw, silhouetted on rooftops, dogs howling at clouds as though against some necromancer's spell as canines swirled by in the river in the street, heads erect from the surface.

Curling on the couch, we watched water streak the glass and dogs spin through the night. They were being drowned by forces beyond our control, martyred to things unseen.

You should know: my girlfriend is somnolescent. When she sleeps she's dead as rock. Only water can wake her. Alarms don't work, nor thunder and lightning.

Enraptured by rivulets on the glass and the silver sound of the river through the street, we gave ourselves over to our own damp pastime. When I woke she was gone. Clothes on the floor in mock flight: pants legs in mid-sprint fold toward the door, and the arms of her cream blouse in a Y of fright as if, caught by some horror, she combusted into the floor.

Next morning, the investigating detectives shook their heads and laughed. Twins but for their hair—one had none, the other a lot—the same smashed bulldog face hung from the fronts of their heads like trashed party masks.

"Women, and people, don't vanish into thin air," the bald one grunted, chewing a hairpin. I didn't notice the pin when they came in, wondered if it was my girlfriend's. Rooting through our belongings, drawers, closets and used-underwear hamper (the bald one lingered in nipping pungence, as if hunting some ripe clue), they found nothing. They overturned my silk screener and surf-apparel forging equipment, thinking them components of some elaborate cotton press. (Aquasilver and Hog Dog ponchos sold the best, talismans from the days of ozone.) "And if they do, they leave something."

I nodded to the clothes on the floor. "She left those. She was wearing them when she vanished."

"You sound so sure, Ace. Why?"

"Would she leave naked?"

"All those silk asswraps in the closet are yours?"

The detective with hair didn't laugh so much as grin by violent slurping, hocked into my sink. "Too skinny for those skirts. Look at his little legs."

They looked at my legs. I crossed them and leaned against the hall door. "I went through her clothes," I said carefully. "None missing."

The hairy detective's eyebrows arched in delight: "You mean you know your girlfriend's wardrobe by heart?"

The Dogs

I turned to the bald one, now seeming more of an ally if because less of a dick. "The door was bolted from inside. Windows locked."

A laugh of amused condescension came from his haired partner.

"So: she just disappeared," the bald detective said.

"Another possibility?"

Scrunching his eyes, he put balled fist to chin, stared at the floor a minute: "You got a cellar door?"

"It's an apartment. No."

"What do you mean, 'No.'" He thrust an enormous knuckle to my breastbone. He pushed me to the couch, where I mingled with my girlfriend the night before, and shoved me down. "You hiding something?"

"Of course not."

"Billy," the bald one said. "Keep an eye on this slick ricket. I'm checking exit-entrance contingencies."

I heard him in the bedroom, hallway, and bathroom kicking things he examined five minutes earlier. Glass shattered, my hatchet-fin trophy (imitation).

Billy, the detective with hair, walked to the window. Pale light through storm clouds glazed his face. Not staring out so much as in, as if viewing a diorama of disaster scenarios, he passively scanned the waterlogged avenue. Red water braided through the gutter, caressing the swollen and fissured asphalt. "No trace of the dogs," he said quietly, touching pinky knuckle to the glass. "It's like they never were."

I said nothing, listening to the hiss and squeal of the shower-head turned on in my bathroom, surely without the curtain drawn. Medicine cabinet slammed open, bottles and razors jittered onto tile, more shattering glass (the drinking glass in which I soaked my toothbrush in a tincture of bleach and distilled H2O). And then, after a curiously long silence and a zipper's growl, the roar of a column of urine into my toilet, the swish and sizzle of the stream aimed around the bowl and through the center pool and beyond the rim. The bathroom door slammed open then closed. The bald detective sauntered into the kitchen, a tiny stove and sink set on parquet in the living room. Instead of washing his hands, he wiped them on the stove mittens. He smeared a German roach along the rim of the sink with his palm, wiped it on the stove mittens, too. Then he washed his hands in the sink, gently patting them dry on his slacks.

"Lavish place you got here," he observed. "You and your girl grease each other into that bed?"

"It's small," I said. "But cheap."

"With a view of money like that," he said, "no wonder she left."

"She vanished."

"One word for it. Poof," he said, hand blooming in the air.

"She didn't leave me." They grinned, and outside my window a thick red rain battered the concrete and leaves of the potted trees along the street. After a silence, and a hard rattle-burst of drops against the glass, the roof dogs set to howling. "She disappeared, and if you can't figure how," I said, "I'll have to hire someone who can."

My boldness shriveled in their stares.

The bald one turned to the window. "Billy," he said to his partner. "What do you think of these acid rain squalls? More and more unpredictable, huh?"

They exchanged glances. "Violent *and* unpredictable," Billy said, throwing me a sidelong glare. "Can't tell when they'll hit.

The Dogs

Crazy. And *un*predictable. They make people do things, you know, Ron. The crime rate goes through the roof this time a' year. Acid goes to people's heads. Family kill each other. Lovers kill each other. Then, when they regain their senses, they try to cover it up."

They watched me.

"Some," Billy went on, "don't even realize they murdered some-one. The acid fumes make them forget. Sometimes only we can serve as memory-jumpers, by collecting evidence and showing it to them. In a court of law."

Ron, the bald one, grunted. "It's a crying shame."

I crossed my legs. Uncrossed them. "Where could all those dogs have gone?"

Billy said: "The same place those missing family members go— husbands, mothers, girlfriends."

"Brothers."

"Daughters."

"Family friends. Grandmas."

"Dogs."

I waited for them to tell me.

"You don't know?" they said.

"Why would I know?"

"Why would he know," Ron asked Billy. "Huh? Why would *he* know?"

"Don't know," Billy said. "Maybe he's too *smart* to know. Maybe he isn't."

They looked through the suddenly calm air to two silos on the horizon, beyond the end of the boulevard that led past my apartment to the bay. The silos marked the western edge of town and the beginning of the turbid, cold ocean and a stretch of dunes and outmoded mines.

"I'll tell you where they are," Ron told me: "Under investigation, just like you."

Billy, in a contemplative mood, freed from the repartee, stood staring out the glass. "What did you and your girlfriend see through this window?"

"Dogs," I said, "floating."

"Of course," he nodded. "And you sat with her, here, and watched—" he moved his hand slowly, palm down, from one side of the window to the other, a dog floating calmly by.

"Yes—"

"And touched her. Felt her—"

"What's that have to do with—"

"Answer the question," Ron hissed. He rooted casually through the freezer. Closing it, he grabbed a broom from the corner. He thrust its handle tip to the floor, and into the cabinets over the sink, a sadistic dentist probing for caries to my nerve.

"Yes," I said to Billy. "I touched her."

"Here," Billy said, blessing.

"There."

Billy nodded with slow savor, as if rolling the sole clue he needed along his tongue. "So strange," he said, staring out the glass, "the way people touch each other. Magnetic fields—like squids. Here we are, we've touched you, and it'll affect you, but we don't know how yet. Did you love her?"

"What do you mean?"

"What do I mean?" Billy asked Ron.

"What does he mean?" Ron stabbed the broom through the

back plaster of a cabinet. He stared at me. "He means, when you greased her into that bed, did you grease any parts especially tender, he means."

Ron, seeing no one would laugh, roved the broom through the cabinets explosively, tore cans and foodstuffs onto the parquet.

Billy moved to my desk. Lifting a small snow globe from the papers, he peered into its divided hemispheres, one a tableau of Santa kneeled amid a group of jubilant styrene children, the other a nightscape of burnt homes and skeleton-strewn stones. Billy grinned at Santa Claus and shook the globe to make it snow. Through swirling cellophane motes he noticed the bones side.

He looked at me. "What the fuck is this?"

"Where could those dogs have gone?" I said quickly.

Billy cradled the paperweight like he might thrust it through my eye. "What's the idea?"

"Man's Faces, I guess." The globe said this itself, on a plaque at its base.

"A sick joke?"

Ron tore the last cabinet door from its hinges and tossed it on the cans on the parquet, yawned. "No alternative entrances in cabinets or floor," he said. He speared the broom into the ceiling. Washes of dust came from the plaster. He pronounced officiously, "No contingencies in roof," snapping the broom on his knee.

Billy, who'd been quietly examining me, said, "You're the bastard who killed those dogs."

"What?"

"Dogs," he said.

"They were killed?"

"What do you think 'happened?' God's 'vengeance?' Please," he said. "It's bastards like you that make the world hell."

"What?" I said.

"The flood was your fault," Billy said.

"How could I have caused the flood? I'm a normal man."

Billy thinned his eyes. "Sabotage."

"Of what?"

He stepped forward. "*You* tell *me*."

"No," I said. "I mean," I said, "I have no idea."

Watching me, he put the globe to my nose. "Where's the *good*?"

It shattered against the wall; glass and children's parts flew through the room.

"Where's the good in a flood? Or in my girlfriend vanishing?" I shouted. "Did I cause that?"

"You confess?"

"I profess, gentleman, you're the brightest radiation twins I ever met."

Billy lunged but his partner, there anyway, swung the handle of the broom into my eye.

They left in the early afternoon. The streets were dry. They left me with their cards, in the sides of my mouth, as I fought from the bedframe they tied me to with her clothes. As they left they told me they'd get her abductor—who was me. A matter of compiling the evidence or, they said, faking it. "Don't worry, Ace. We'll solve your case."

They left me with her pants—they took her blouses, sandals, to their wives. I wore her pants around my neck and stared through the glass, listening to the silence that follows rain.

I heard a howl. On the building across the street a dog, tall and black, watched me. It lashed its tail against the sky, crying accusations, each slowly falling to the broken street past my closed window.

Night Bowls

Hot, he watches skaters return reluctant through the gold lot to their cars, souls flowing over concrete still. His glides down concave as he steers truck through the night, used-car lot flood-lamps and lightboxes of *Quick Service* restaurants in his eyes, his laminate pine sliding still. Burger smell fumes from his knuckles on the wheel.

Scoop the rot, dice, fry the right time. Fry them right.

Fries right and graduate to cheese—fries, meat—shakes, meat man: the managers make eighty grand.

He tries so hard with the fries. Can't get them. Breaching from the hissing canola they are dark. The managers watch him with smiles, speaking quietly. Meat men watch him with suspicion; watch his thumby fingers with a total solace.

In the morning, pour half a gallon of cleanser on the patio. Scrape until it's good.

Cashier girls brew coffee in aluminum tubs in the drive-thru.

They never see him.

He rises in dark with streetlamps cressets in the palace mist, and when he moves into the orange air itching for Lucky Strike, his roommate Jude is on the porch, saying "Tonight tarot" through smoke.

The landlord roses are delicate silhouettes on the thin garage.

He and Jude read the future. A show about surfing vampires who ride moonlit waves, feast on teens, and other cable shows with satisfying ocular fever. A dark woman comes. Opportunity will bring risk. The hangman hangs on your corner.

The vampire surfers glaze the coffee table and yucca ashtray, comforting burger trash.

He scrapes sizzling cheese from the steel. The cheese caramelizes web across the metal. He pries, orders screech. Iceberg crisp over beef, the grass of a Babylonian arbor. The pillared slivers of tomatoes are stamens of charmed fungi. "Cheeseburger," "hamburger," "three grilled cheese" comes the voice of the window girl.

In his room he watches headlights sweep ceiling, thinks of the bowls and their continual cement.

He'll get the fries. He'll master shakes. Make manager, meat, eighty grand. A dark woman is coming. He'll buy her a home with roses along a multi-car garage.

If he can't, the night bowls, in the street the color of cheese when it crystals.

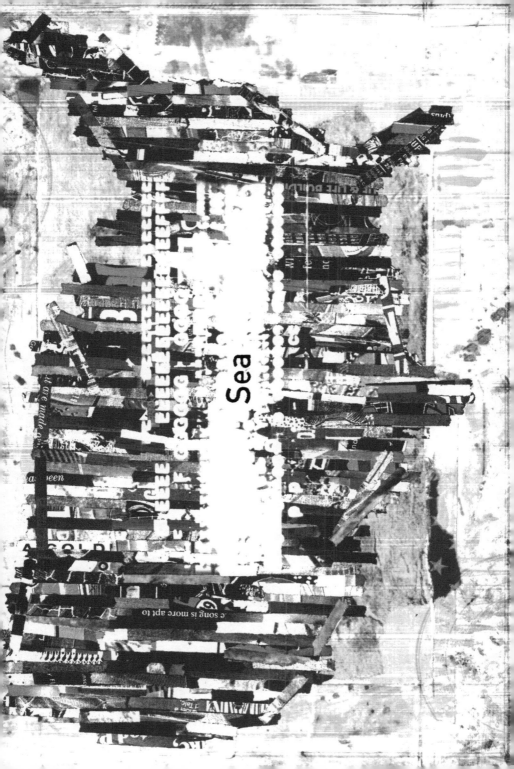

Sea

RON

I bring her melted cookie. Her eyes shine.

She stares.

She comes in my van.

SYBIL

Ron comes. I kiss him at the store.

Take me. Ron, these days are hot. The sweat . . .

LOST AMERICANS

JACK

It sheathes to you. I watch her and Ron. Buy wax. Watch how they

RON

I want out of here. Take me, she says between boards. Bell jingles; she nips my ear. *After this*, she says, grips me, *let's get out of here.*

She is serving her customer. Tall Jack, watching me through the fiberglass.

JACK

I walk the point along the cobbles and rocks. Walk the sand. I mark what's mine, the time till tide. I am old, younger than you; I guard it, I won't let go, the authority I hold in the line.

The others watch me; they're wary. They drift and I spray their eyes.

Never leave this point. Watch those who come. Young ones cut in. They learn, some stay as long as I, through crisp nights of mist when the cold calls the roar of tide and the Rincon derricks sing their dark, far steel.

Sea

You want her.

SYBIL

Ron.

He likes me, I think.

Loves me I think.

In those rocks, he says. Suck his smoke.

Doze, see moon through rock. Dead-fish smell of sea. Thinking: do I need him, like this, do I like me?

Depends?

Does *he* like *me*?

JACK

I pass a cave in the moon.

I hear the birds cry.

Whisper.

She says, *Jack. You're not* that *big.*
Could be your father, I grin, touching.
Her eyes shine, cisterns. Little fingers tinker.
Will you take me? Jack?

Where?

SYBIL

Will you? I told Ron.

You know, he said, all smirk. He put his mouth to mine. He grabbed me.

RON

She comes in the rocks. (Ron, you're *the Don.*) She comes, I do. We'll finish in these rocks, I tell her, Sybil, we'll. We will lock . . . in these rocks and stay.

She's looking at the night. She holds her knees, her spine the shadow of dunes.

I sleep.

———

Sea

JACK

You've been watching me.
Jack.
Here? Come, I pull, into those rocks—a sec.
I know, she says, *those jetty rocks.*
Well?
Well—
No, she tells the sea. *You know I'm wrong. You're not . . . it.*

I hate them.

I hate them coming.

Kook: in your glistened Chevy, your mail-order suit, in my sea with new epoxy Glider.

Come.

Where?

Come, I beg.

Where?

Where? I say.

Yes, she says, *Jack. Where?*

She stares out to sea.

SYBIL

Ron!

God.

Ron . . .

God!!

RON

We eat dogs from plastic. Cold, good. Hot: good too. We eat 'em and ride line. Eat and ablute our body. Eat and drink and slide.

Ron, her belly on my ear. I hear sea and smell salt.

Ron, she whispers.

Ron . . .

SHE TALKS AND TALKS. STEAM FILLS THE KITCHEN. IT CLINGS TO THE wall and moistens her skin. It mists her eyes as Mitchel eats her hot food with an absent smile.

Through the window, resting over the boiling water, she looks at the city of parallelograms in the fading light. The el rattles the pane; steel wheels screech like glass being scratched.

The moon has risen. Confused ascents and descents of concrete stop at her window. She meets the bank tower's insisting glare; high on its metallized blue, a sign for loans tells her to *SIGN AND DRIVE!* A long trail of zeroes of an odometer of pleased customers lines the ledge like suicides or baby moons.

She thinks of Markus somewhere in that city, with a woman who doesn't talk and talk about things he can't stand.

Does he think of her? Does he think of her in her box with her dead man?

Mitchel watches her clean.

She thinks of Marcus across the Guatemalan grocery stores crowded in the evening dark below the el; across their marimba and tinkling fluorescence and their chill, pork air flooding through aisles of expired anise and fruit, she feels him.

Does he feel her through the furor, through the glowing towers? Her body? As she was?

She kisses Mitchel.

An End of War

A MAN NAMED SAVIOR JUAN ENDED WAR, LEGEND HAD IT. RUMOR come down from the days of free information had his birth name as Jon Wexler or James Samson, engineers in the Research and Development Lab of a transnational corporation who worked to produce low-frequency electromagnetic transmitters inducing vermin to starve. The instrument made frequencies with resonance in hypothalamus, to gridlock hunger; the pests eliminated themseves from basements and home gardens.

The Savior of Man, by the legend, worked with the signals until ions chained instincts to metabolism. He induced rhesus not to fight, or if they did, to die.

The Savior went rogue. Backed by a cadre of angel investors, he perfected the technique while the corporation and the governments of the world hunted him. With the help of his investors a model of the transmitter, streaming from the telecom satellite armadas, inundated the globe.

T-cells corroded nerves and arterioles. The angered individual found a way to calm himself, or liquefied.

The first to fall victim to the device were radio and television shock jocks. Years after inception, their last broadcasts played at commemorative holidays to remind us of the rage that consumed humanity before enduring calm. Unable to stifle their anger, hitherto lucrative, the jocks dissolved on screen and on air before their awed studio audiences.

Armageddon: the streets flooded with liquescent people. As stocks fell, Savior Juan's investors bought corporate titans and government equity, declared themselves the Fathers of Peace and assumed rule of a contented mankind with an eye to quarterly gain.

The dynasties of the Fathers of Peace directed industry. They turned the first-world militaries into one global R and D net to make conveniences they sold to humanity at good, healthy prices. Peace Corp wrought unprecedented margin. Savior Juan disappeared under shrouded circumstances.

Ingenuity, cut and honed, birthed probes capable of seventy percent the speed of light. The probes scoured the galaxy for venture.

The FOP thrived in this new epoch of innovation and unrelenting calm. They built crystal submarine palaces in the Mariana Trench, villas on the slopes of Half Dome in Yosemite. They bought midtown Manhattan and ensconced headquarters for the two incestuous houses of the Descendants of Peace in Rockefeller Center and the Empire State Building.

Man entered a genetic sieve. The radiation ensured trouble for the strong-minded but survival of the bovine. The stressful audits of corporate accounting, high-demand manufacture, killed all but the cool. A mellow rocket assembler with a good record of fitting chill rings cut a pinky and at the surging adrenaline was chutney on the tile. An hour found an efficient replacement at his post.

An End of War

We fitted. We pressed into the psychic criteria like knives into fat, two hours sleep enough for cognitive loads at nine-percent mental use. We sleekened into our narrow range.

The Families of Peace looked on from verandas.

They needed to subvert the radiation that cut into their freedom. They installed cages of silver in the roofs of their apartments. The silver conductivity dampened the raining signal. (Secretly indulging, they hated.)

They became addicted, in time. Within domes of covert pleasure, a millennium of termite urge swarmed from their sacral spine. Vivisecting the weak among them selected for the thirsty. They tortured pets, drank blood. They thrived, as in the streets of the crystal cities humans didn't touch, sliding on the metro on an efficient film of speech trimmed into eyebrow crimp and tightened mouth. We didn't know scowl, lost to time as anal domination by Norsemen. Flat squint, meaningless waiting stare (idling between instructions), all we needed.

Asteroids fell upon the supercities. Bogotá, Buenos Aires and the Falkland Islands were craters of char. New York stood, gratered. The satellites streaked the sky like seraphim falling from their station. Into the ash at evening the descendants of the FOP walked onto cool balcony. They allowed their thirst to open in the night air.

We didn't sense the lack of spell.

The Children of Peace came into the streets with bolt-cutters and scythes. The new equanimity of the race won: we produced precision drill bits without hesitating as we went into the night.

The Dead Kingdom

SHE CRAVED AMERICAN SUCCESS.

Her theory: you worked, you success. You worked enough that obstructions blew from your path with momentum (money). You worked until gold sprouted from the mulch you made of your soul. Avaricious roots leached you, and from the useless you a bouquet of American gold—the shit of you, the waste, inefficiency, the sideline dream, pure. Once she tried to be a poet.

When she remembered this as she lay in bed, Nada felt the wild words she'd mashed under transduction cascades turn in her. Parsed syllable in her deep like limb of murdered children. Consonants, splintered bone of morpheme, cut her tongue. Swallowed vowels discharged gas into her throat. Renegades, tight in her shoulders, kept her from sleep. She trudged over them toward her gold dream.

Though he saw her views on career, still Clarence drew. In the library he walked up and down the aisles hunting frayed, splintered binding, portraits of lithograph silver. He smelled the stale, earth smell of the spines. In a carrel at the end of the aisle he drew until his eyes were clinkered coal. He took the book home, hiding in it from her dream.

He drew until every photographic line, the lines of unknown faces, filled him. The faces of dead strangers opened their eyes inside his throat. He stared at the photos through the night and drew, and sweated, and felt the world lift from him.

He showered. He rode to Hotel Goldenwest.

"Do doodles. *Go.* Come at two to do *real* work," Imran told him, elbows on the veined Formica. "I ask you to save your doodles for breaks, smoke. Your time."

Clare laid his pen down and looked out the entrance.

In the rain, the traffic eyes glittering in rivers, tourists made their way to the Kingdom.

Nada slammed a door. "Mister Portraiteer."

They howled.

He held her.

"Tell me you love me," she said.

He did.

"Think life will split the fruits?"

Clare watched Imran with level disinterest. He shot back a, "Yes."

"You think this life is for you?"

"Who else?"

The Dead Kingdom

Imran was silent. "A customer," he said toward the lithe lady who scissored to the counter. With a long stare at her, he dissolved into his office.

Clare confronted him: "You don't like me."
"Would I?"
"Want to talk about it?"
"You Americans *love* talk." Imran gathered receipts. Pillars from the glass of the roof, other hotel orifices, deep, strangulated purple. "Don't you?"
Noons they smoked together by the turquoise pool at the back of the hotel. Imran gave him Reds. They let the smoke drift in women's hair across their eyes. The chaise longues faced an interval in the garish, themed hotels, a field of pump skeletons.
Angels rose at noon from their sentries in the Kingdom. Their fiberglass bodies and trumpets gleamed climbing the wires to the tor.
Imran caught Clare watching them. The leaves of gold hid the curled razor, the cameras on pilings, the alp, in the center. It was a nimbused idol. "You want to go."
"Man," Clare said.
"You were staring with your hungry eye." Imran watched the eucalyptus: a wall of seamless flame between him and a complete peace of mind. "Give me those receipts. Go."

She began third-year rotations when he started to draw tourists at the Kingdom. If she didn't impress, she'd end a pediatrician drowning in Medicare. An attending with a girthy neck offered a letter. He offered a whiskey.

Her eyes ached. The luminous diseases clogged her channels, his squat fingers, gently, with a certainty that touched a pleasure, turning her from the images.

Her hands were blistered with sanitizer eczema. Some nights she forgot to eat, slid by his desk into unconsciousness.

"What is it?"

"No," she said.

He went to his desk, to the eyes.

The one invented asepsis; this one, a cardiothoracic surgeon (the first in Russia), weathered Stalin and Kruschev's turbulent retirement as a doctor up in the Party.

"The dumb ones become doctors," the woman said, matter of fact (Nada wilting, just slightly (it was routine)), the emerald eyes on him those of an esurient lion.

She taught at her school. An atheist and biophysicist exploring the cradles of the mechanisms.

"Your drawings," she said, once. "They're good."

She gave him long hugs when welcoming him on the porch of the Craftsman cottage.

She gave him succinct hugs when he left.

The departing hug, congratulatory—they *had held*, through her stories and his vacated listening, strong.

The churches of the towns found him. He was eighteen then.

The Dead Kingdom

He filled the hours of the winter his father died with the community christs, to keep what had killed his father from opening in him. The sermons on his incineration, or Jesus' endless generosity until you died, blew cool sealant over the cracks in the dark egg.

They didn't seem to him to have questions. They assigned passages of the Book to him. He found two saviors in it. One was snide; he liked this Christ. There was another one.

"You will be salted with fire."

"The angels shall come, and cast you into the furnace: you will wail."

"Let the dead bury the dead."

When they discovered his father they told him: peace was his. When he told him he shot himself in the throat, they said: Pray. God. They could not explain—the turns in the subdued and wandering logic of their tales suggested nothing was for it. But they told him, their eyes now down, pray.

When he couldn't sleep he walked through the city.

Spritzing trucks covered the city. A carcinogenic mist, with a cold indifferent citrus, came from the cement like souls. It cooled him.

He drew the dim façades. The blue neon compass burned in the wall of the Mason Lodge. The homeless hunched in the yolk streetlight moving into arbors along the rail. A makeshift Merengue club in a body shop: he watched the Latinos runneling over the blinking floor. Along the streets he held a line, a gliding silhouette.

Colts and spurs effulgent, his sweaty, dirty jeans charcoal strokes through the overbright crowd, the gunslinger moved with stealth through the tourists. Clare had drawn portraits in Old New Orleans a month before he heard of him. It was rumored he fled through murals with a demon ease, felinely slid through the labyrinths of corridor and forests of shadow cast by attractions. The hunting party of undercover detectives grew.

He seemed to have appeared when the first children went.

Rare afternoons, Clare heard the vendors and portrait artists say, he donned a rakish vest, silk and white as his sombrero, but stained with the red dust on his boots. He traversed the hundred kingdoms, stopping to stare at the sun, checking the time until the crowd thinned and he had to shelter.

One dusk, he was caught on camera. He kneeled at the brink of Jade Falls, in the center of the park, cupped hands into the yellow bell of water into a pool. Bringing the cold chlorine to his mouth he drank deeply. Security came in a minute but he was gone.

No one knew where—not even those who saw him go. The tourists at the railing snapped photos of the gunslinger and then argued: a Quebecois saw him dash over the lip into shady Pioneer Forest. Others claimed he tore off his boots and swam the lagoon's curry to Lost Children's Isle. The security men ran fingers through their hair, staring over the surface of churned carotene in the low sun. Excited children clambering on rocks on the island, their screams loud over the water, looked at the white steamboat that whistled. Tiers lit by oil lanterns glistened calmly in a cake of white pine.

Foreign to the tan Californians, the gunslinger was always discerned in the crowd. His raw physiognomy under the sombrero was ruthless. Wind harsher than the breezes here, laden as they were with marine moisture, had aged him prematurely. Incipient cancers specked his face, his eyes kinked at their sides though he could not have been twenty-one.

The first girl vanished from the Triassic Train.

The Junior Astronaut, on a lone voyage in the Sky Ships, parents clapping at the rail, was snatched away in his slow migration to the Emerald Chateau across the sky.

Next two teens.

Their parents left them playing in Babylon while they got lemon ice. The girls did not emerge from the vines when their parents screamed.

The gunslinger stood staring into a mirror pool, light webs menacing him under his sombrero, minutes after the girls descended into the crevices of the ruins.

Initially corporate requested the costumed rustler for questioning, but the sheriffs and gunhands of Lincoln, New Mexico—two zones east of Babylon—did not know the strange man staring with a wistful look into his image, the tourist stream forking around him on the video, ants around a coal.

Rumors of sightings passed among the crews, toy vendors, popcorn men and sugar sculptors. He moved in smooth silence through the visitors, colts and belts burning, jeans dark on the ecstatic color.

Clare sat at his easel in Old New Orleans twelve hours a day. He drew the sunburnt tourists who stopped into the shade on their way to adventures. Stone-eyed east coast Americans; slack-faced west coasters; ice-gazed Australians, Austrians, and Eastern Europeans. Coal-eyed Chinese, Nigerians, Senegals. You couldn't see what you wanted unless you looked when they weren't. You caught it after futile minutes of chiseling at their features, as they turned, in vulnerable unpoised stare. Their thin perspirant cellophaned them while they stared dreamily at the glaciers of the Alp rising above. In an instant, you saw who they were and let them pass.

The hot Santanas whistled through the townhouses. They stung his eyes as he drew.

His employer, and co-owner of the company, Roger Thorn, extracted from every chrysalis of face an ideal. Thorn's pastel sucked fat from cheekbone ineffably, excavating hidden structure.

Thorn saw that Clare's strength lay in rendering the microscopic brutalities suffered in a life, which nestled around the eyes. But he saved the wrinkled customers for himself.

He hired the young man on his portfolio strength—photographic detail produced obsessively through hours of insomnia. He regretted the decision. Nearly every portrait Clare started ended smudged or incomplete.

Thorn told Clare to study one of his finest works, an obese child with a gleaming look.

Clare drew it ninety-seven times.

When Clare posted the final version at his easel, easel, tourists diverted towards it. The tourists wanted that polish; they sensed a chance at eternity. Having themselves laminated into the Enchanted Kingdom's fake vellum, the tourists would become deathless as the rat king's vinyl stare.

In real time, without the expansive quiet of the night to work in, he couldn't stray from his tourists' eyes without meltdown. Fanning the planes of their cheeks with charcoal brought a naked feeling. He rappelled cheeks until he locked his lines to something in the pupil. He dug at their eyes for an hour as he tried to do this, in the echoing 19th-century Louisiana port, under the derisive stares of the artists.

"Practice." Thorn guided a visibly distressed customer away from his easel.

Nada silently shoved past him to bed. Through her eyes, the eyes her mother gave her, he saw a fey boy kneeling over his image in a pool of scum, staring for the entrance to success. He continued to draw rotogravure.

"What is it?"

She said nothing.

"What?" he said.

The December cold accented the fragrance of the churros.

Some days he stared into the plumes of smoke over the carts and remembered what this park had meant to him.

The bright saloons, and Enchanted Castle, the prim, All-American storefronts of Hometown, U.S.A., and the friendly copyrighted characters waiting, to Clare, formed an authentic family. To the father who brought him here once after his mother died, growing irritable as the day ground on, they were macerating America with their insect saliva, eroding its heroes: Geronimo, Jesse James, John C. Fremont, William Tecumseh Sherman, Stonewall Jackson, and General Robert Lee and (in a bath of seraphic beam) Commander George Washington.

The faces of Red Rascal, the oval-eyed Snakey Jake, and famed and charismatic rodent, King Jimney, immaculately would carve themselves into a mountain larger than Denali, his father said, the brooding judgment of his fundamentalist blood possessing him as they crept through the lot.

Clare loved the park.

She pinned him. His reflex was to get weird, to scramble her verbal advantage. He fuzzed metaphors, encrypted his insults to soften her diction.

"You want me to be a Kinko's bitch?" he said. "I could be the faxboy in admin; maybe they'll give us discount lunches in your school Café." She stared. She decoded. He gripped her throat somehow.

The contempt became routine. Once he had sliced to the inadequacy, and she had winced, muted the way her mother's ingenious control quieted her, she began hardening. He had to give more thrust to cut.

He discussed his soul.

"What is your soul's work?" she asked, finally. A physician comported, tensed shoulders the clue he'd cut. "What have you got, for your unique nightmare?"

His answer he chose not to share.

They held each other. A light bathed his cold inner well—a lit-wishpool light.

"Tell me you love me," she said.

He did.

The cheese peppers jeered. The piroshkis, inseminated with honey, burst so hot in his mouth they promised coming cost.

He savored. The mother stood, arms folded, in his mind, smiling. Try, she said.

He drew Nada.

The Dead Kingdom

The plan: to awe her. He pictured her standing at the portraits, the romantic act sedimenting their love. And the collection would bring Success—galleries, money.

In bed, Clare asked: "Do you think the dead hear?"

"I don't think about the dead." Nada rolled to him.

"Think about them.

"I just wonder if they hear us," he said.

She said, "I kind of feel dead."

"If they do, don't they talk," he said. "I think they do and, that's all they—or, sleep. Or."

The ass division he clenched, an imperiled rock climber.

"What?" she said.

"They wait."

He drew magazine covers of supermodels to hone the Thorn technique. The pale acid of their anemia ate the faces he preferred, in his head (their mouths opened in wails).

Fifteen children dissipated into the decorative cement. He knew he had pushed them somehow into the cracks.

Thorn watched him work on an old European woman. Poor technique, he said. Clare slowly circled her leached iris, not to touch its core, feeling he was spinning a coal. Just as he let the lines shoot, radiant, from the ducts over her cheekbones and drapery eye, Thorn told him softly, You'll never get structure. You'll never achieve semblance, that way.

Clare put down the pen. Pastel, Thorn said. It allows correction.

He told Clare again to start distant from the eyes with the universal ratios. To move inward through tracking of this architecture to the rosette around the pupil, which he could add last as a relish to the crisp design.

He tried with the woman. When he got to the eyes nothing was left in him. He used it all in the trek across the continents of her skull. He Pangeaed them, pinned the topographics with shining, hard pupils, but it came out gelid.

"Good," Thorn said. "Just practice."

With young, ecstatic tourists he was in even less control. They had no eyes to start with. In their gloss were two diodes that flicked with social procedure, unpowered screens when they sat and looked at him. Occasionally a friend made them laugh and the screens sparked, the face took the creases of soul, then smoothed immediately.

He moved their features into approximate order like the append-ages of a cumbersome doll without screws or direction, veering his way through methods.

"Yes," Thorn said.

It came, then. He drew tourists with ease. The rims of hangdog conjunctivitis lent a red leer, the lips lined in chocolate he rendered with a calm authority. He assembled the jumble, all the roundings and shines, their eyes not holding them down for him.

The tourists' eyes glistened with fattened anticipation. They could not wait to see what he'd done, themselves memorialized within gilt bounds, intertwined with the park.

He didn't crave the dead. He felt agile. He was sallow. His body had become wire. Money. The money accrued in the hole.

Nada's portraits melded. Every sketch became the one before, receding further from him; her features sunk into slop as tourists crystallized cleanly across the parchment.

They didn't talk. She stayed at the research lab (she stayed out).

The Dead Kingdom

If he were drawing the dead he wouldn't care. He couldn't. The tourists depleted him. When she did come home the labyrinth guided: he kissed her. They ate. She went to bed. She was gone when he woke.

Corporate representatives came through the kingdoms one winter afternoon. They brought papers for employees to sign: a confidentiality agreement that stated no employee would engage in hearsay about the events, or the rustler. *If* any employee *did* engage in hearsay, they would face the hardened in-house attorneys and suffer punishment to the fullest extent of the law.

He made Portrait Artist of the Quarter. A drawing of his, the corporate rep who sat for a drawing after distributing the agreement, sat in the Talent Cupboard flanked by Thorn pieces.

Nada moved down a hall in the hospital.

She had been working 28 hours. Benzedrine simmered in her, her sight flickered whitely, covered in a film of bacterial feel. The black hole of her face in the floor of polished cement became Clare's face. His face became the mouth of his hole.

A staccato of heels. The hair on her neck rose thinking of professional smiles, in the dead fluorescence, electrostatically coercing her to smile.

She lowered through the floor into his hole. She found herself somewhere hot. The goosesteps quieted, mute light sifting above her.

He smelled acrid. Whiffs had come before but she'd never been *inside. Clare,* she incanted, to dispel some rising terror, to remind herself of something. She breathed, lowering into his acceptance of her. The glue was his acceptance. The thought of him became a warm bed.

She saw eyes, then: they reached as far as the light went. They began to move, aglitter. They came and put her face to theirs. They imprinted the clay with their smiles.

Shocked at the noise she'd made, three doctors glanced down the scarred silver hall.

From a vent in her kind men poured. She saw hard chins and slick demeanors ascending. She was comforted when she remembered all those inviting grins that she had stored in her like genies.

They coaxed spurts of dopamine from the grayness, possibility.

The sea of eyes of men valiantly fought the faces of the dead.

Her mother answered. The mother interrupted herself two minutes into the monologue about the incompetence of their cleaner—a Serbian refugee she took pity on *one too many times*. Her instincts activated. She said: "How's he?"

"He," the closest she let him come. She used "the boyfriend". As "the" he was a blender, functioned object.

Nada cried.

"Some swim. Some fly. Some live, Nadezhda. Some don't."

"Come," the mother said. "Rest, piroshki."

"With butter," Nada said. "Or chemical shit."

"Butter," lied the mother.

The Dead Kingdom

One evening at closing, Clare found the gunslinger sitting in front of his easel.

The young man had starvation and violence in his crimson eyes. "Draw me. *Quick*," he said.

The portrait was magic. The next night he came back, revitalized. His guns shone hot. He resembled the portrait Clare drew: tanned skin; calm, knowing stare.

He bought another, and seemed more at ease when Clare drew him the second time. Clare asked his name.

"Billy Bonney."

"Clarence."

"*Mucho gusto.*"

The man lit a cigarette, watching the tourist flow through the lamps of New Orleans.

Billy the Kid came each night. Every rendering strengthened him. He grew cockier. Clare found the portraits honed his focus. The drawings held the vigor of the dead. He studied them with a satisfaction before handing them over.

Clare drew the Kid any chance he could. On slow afternoons, sent for a shipment of portrait frames at the employee entrance, he rested on a ledge at the back of the Mayan Temple, sketching him from memory.

The Kid introduced friends to his easel. Strange slaves, marquises, pirates, monastics in vows of silence who nodded eagerly at the drawings Clare did, they came from unknown zones of the park.

The artists watched with envy as Clare dumped Billy's silver dollars on the counter at close.

He noticed the faces he drew pressing daily through New

Orleans. Conquistadors and plantation owners, failed bank men. They peered into the Glass Slipper souvenir hut, marveled with tourists at the intricate castles, the crystal of copyrighted cartoons.

"Your friends leave their kingdoms a lot," Clare told Billy.

"They've put in their time."

"Where do the children go?" Clare said.

"Nowhere they don't want to."

"How do you know?"

"Disappeared?" asked the Kid.

"No."

The Kid grinned: "You don't want to."

Clare had cupboards of her. A cupboard of deglutened pasta, placemats of works by Schiele (he hated Schiele). Her breath came out at him, a warm, yogurt odor from the dark that brought memories. The cupboards stocked with foods she bought, and their tastes. A glimpse of her small feet on the bed along the hall while he washed dishes. He sprayed the cupboards with citric bleach.

He kept good companions with his portraiture. Etching lines, he thought of her. In *Duck Duck Goose* cadence, he whispered, eyes following the ink labyrinths on the desk, as he tapped her shoulder, "Fuck you."

She came back. She cried. They cried. "I *love* you." He cried: after an interminable week she became anxious, then cruel. He sent her pastels of the alp, its slopes on the sky like turquoise tile. Notes of the visual poetry of the glints on rails and the pools of hydrochlorate used to sterilize the common paths and scrub the Kingdom to its gleaming bones.

She left him the Kingdom. The colors of the Grand Carousel,

kaleidoscopic in the dark; the lamps licking with tongues of flame the rose beds, tikis burning around black faces in the cement.

The dead didn't come all together, he said. The young came through the holes. When they stretched wide with the traffic, the adults passed through. They found paradise, they thought.

Dead wrong, laughed the Kid. This resort was imagineered for visitors, for willing dreamers, not the dead, who could see through the decorative cement to the churning gears.

The mild intruders dried out in the heat. They withdrew to the shady gantries and the alpine caverns. Soft shell creatures pulled from their pool, they had no tolerance for the California heat. They emerged at night, but eventually the sun took the last of their water and they blew away as carapace on the wind.

How no one noticed them, Billy said. "They blew out as they came—until you helped. I knew there was something special in you, soon as I saw you that night, like a crawdad tight in your alley."

The art rooted them to the Kingdom. The image sealed them from the sun, their pastel eyes cauterized embarkation.

Clare tried again: "The girls, and the children, that vanished . . . "

Generous, Billy smirked and said: "I had some time to acquaint myself with new ideas. A Frenchman told me—when one thing comes, another goes the way it came. *Le Chatelier*," the Kid said. "They have a new home."

The dead savored the air. The Mediterranean night coaxed memories from their souls, of walking raw coasts long eaten by the wind, lights in their eyes while they roamed the shadow, down the Kingdom avenues, to Hometown, U.S.A., where candy shops and soda fountains burned furiously.

They ventured into the neon with their portraits.

"This shithole crowds me—I can't quit it,," the Kid confided when they sat behind the employee commissary one afternoon.

Billy squinted into the towers in the sun, visible beyond the concentric chain-link fences. He spat tobacco.

Clare reflexively reassured, "You will," to keep Billy still so he could get a line along his nostril.

"Yeah?" The Kid's eyes had gone homicidal. "I wish I was so sure as you."

Clare traced the masseter nervously.

Billy looked once more at the towers. "You are a man doomed to stick wherever he sits."

Adult tourists began to vanish.

Thorn, stern admiral at the helm of his sinking man-o-war, manned the cash counter stoically. The disconsolate crew clung near him under the saloons and townhouses, watching the dead pour into the alley in brazen gangs.

The Kid scoured the underground tunnels for a way into the sewers.

Below a new moon he went to where the perimeter fence touched the interstate. He threw a tarp over the high barbwire and straddled steel coil with one boot to the retaining wall, car lights beating his sombrero, unable to extract his other boot from the park.

He never tried to leave through the turnstiles. To Clare this seemed the easiest first step. "Too dangerous," he whined. He'd be captured before he made it three rows into the kilometer car lot.

Some unresolved conflict kept him here.

In the afternoon, during the languorous hours when three parades crossed the Kingdom, Thorn passed the time enumerating tourist deaths.

The swimmer drowned on Graduation in a swim to Children's Isle, and the retarded man toppled from the sky on a rainy day.

Henderson and Bill, Thorn's protégés, listened, occasionally challenging small details and adding clarification.

Something in the flowing light off the bayou drew the stories from them. The other artists leaned their elbows on the counter to listen.

"Twenty," Thorn summarized. The artists nodded solemnly, watching the dead bob through the thinning tourists.

Clare said: "Has anyone killed themselves here?"

The cartoon chimeras had their time. As had their disciples.

Clare worked with drive. The dead crammed the Kingdom.

Thorn ordered his artists to refuse service to the dead.

Clare, as a reprisal, made a boycott of the living.

Knowing Thorn would fire him if he handed over antique

Reichsmarks and florins, Clare paid for the portraits with savings. Billy had come to the bottom of his coins.

Billy leaned against a wrought-iron pillar. He looked concerned. "You're hungry, Clare."

Clare thumbed the dun of a Sicilian girl. She watched Billy the Kid uneasily.

"If you got no *plata* for the *jefe*, you best take care."

Clare smiled wan.

"I have them." He indicated the wave of dead coming down the corridor.

Clare signaled for the next in line. An acned Teutonic squire slid into the chair timidly, chainmail clattering.

Clare noticed a guard along the passage. He whispered to Billy: the gunslinger was gone.

As the number of dead grew, old rides and attractions rose. Solomon's Mines, creaking precursor to the cement alp's toboggan race, revived suddenly as a drowning victim coughing to life, its jewel mine chutes coming alive with light and sound one cool winter night. Billy and Clare felt the vibrations from its racing carts through the paving at the alp base, heard the screams of the thrilled riders. The Tower of Horror loomed from the east, a hexagonal bastille with thin scarlet windows leering through the sea of smog drifting from the city on the easterlies. (The Tower had been decommissioned and demolished years before after its scare elevator broke chains and fell ten stories.)

At noon, the angels raced to hide in the caverns of the peak, rolling into the shadow like sunken white eyes.

The Dead Kingdom

Thorn visited Clare's easel.

"Where's the money?"

"What money?"

"It appears you're busier than any artist on the team."

"Strange what you'll see in this Kingdom, Thorn," Clare said.

Their eyes held, but Clare knew now Thorn would not evict him. He had seen the strength of the alliance.

"A shipment is waiting at the bay," Thorn said. "My suggestion: get it."

A soiled light hung over New Orleans. The sun seared into the algal motes. Clare didn't rise. He stared at this half-man, Thorn, a blue-eyed whale hanging in a banquet of krill. Clare hadn't eaten in three days.

"Sir." He pushed through a façade, looking over his shoulder (suddenly grateful to the man for bringing him into this dream), said: "Thank—"

The blank eyes muted him, pushed him on through the townhouse exit.

She came into the courtyard from the sidewalk and registered him without slowing.

"Where were you?" He sat on his voice to make it flat. "I've been waiting."

Tongue pulled bottom lip in a way that was new. "Why didn't you call?"

He hesitated. He hoped she wouldn't notice the faces at the apartment windows that watched him shouting. "Let me in."

A dead face. When she spoke, it was a voice he knew: "I'm sorry."

He waited for her eyes, long neck, to slide into his.

"I'm going?" she said.

He would reach. He didn't, couldn't be shaken away, an insect. "We should walk . . . "

"No."

The dead built. Cathedrals soared. Bridges spanned the river, chalcedony heads along the caissons. Gabrieleños constructed thatch tongvas in the forest shade. Lower Eastside tenements burst out of the Lagoon and tent rafts drifted on the Bayou, silhouetted bandits passionately arguing on the soft candles.

The dead built apartment complexes for the émigrés along the perimeter fence. The river filled with sewage.

Convinced his Kingdom could hold the volume, Clare worked in a fever. Through principle of siphon more dead would come to take the places of those he gave life. When Nada made her entry into the Kingdom, he would give her the tour, as if it were not hers, this realm of power and recreation.

All would pass through death into the turnstiles to find their place as his liege.

The dead celebrated Clare.

Billy brought him into homes. From the penthouses of the high-rise, as Billy the Kid conversed with a turn-of-the-century financier, or a Saint Petersburg aristocrat shot by Bolsheviks, Clare stared at the circle of the river, rippling in wind as it wound like a golden vein through the park.

They ate the feasts at the long tables, the Kid always with a watchful eye on his friend.

The Dead Kingdom

"Do you want me?"

"Of course," Clare said.

"Do you want *just* me?"

"Yes."

"You sound like a machine. Come," she said, guided him from his desk. Her areola a nib in the morning breeze through the French townhouses. They swam in the Baja water that morning. He saw her in the hut, her sweat staining the sheets as she splayed, melted idol.

The artists carved the tips of their pastels silently. They arrayed them in the cardboard with care while waiting for the guests.

A dark form moved at the roofline of Madam Corseau's Leisure Maison. No: the sun hid the white of Billy's sombrero where the wall of the façade rose above ventilator. Coming into a chimney shadow, he locked eyes with Clare, who'd stepped from his alley, and waved him back to his easel.

Henderson, doodling a mauve unicorn riding a wave of hellfire, saw Clare slip around the corner.

Billy came down a balcony. "Don't ask questions. Move."

Clare grabbed his pastel tray instinctively when Billy shoved him into the cobbled passage, drawing a pistol. At the click of hammer Clare's foot caught a stone. He fell against a Napoleon statue, tripped in the direction of the mother stand, nestled between two balconies of moccasins.

Henderson was on his feet with the élan of a young centurion. He slammed a shoulder into Clare, pinned him into a red shutter and held his collar. A bullet tore through his eye.

The artists who had followed Henderson retreated to the counter. With a gelatin gaze, Thorn watched Billy and Clare run toward the exit arch of Old New Orleans.

A Lincoln sedan swung around the souvenir hut and accelerated. They were forced down a blind alley, found themselves against a picturesque watercolor of antebellum ladies and slaves.

The Lincoln rolled slowly into the space. Clare flattened into the mural with heavy pulse, his vision microscopically sharp. He saw the individual strands of steel fiber of the angel wire above him, the pixels of blush of the madame by his eye. Through the tint of the windscreen the security officers smiled. They pushed down the gas.

"Hold me, fucker."

Billy let off two rounds through the tint, and pulled Clare through the wall.

He slipped between fuel drums into the tunnels.

Clare, shocked, watched the car crash halfway through the pink insulation of the façade. They had slipped through the pine without leaving a hole, without resistance. He followed Billy into the subterrain.

When the park had opened that morning at the same time it had opened for seventy years, tourists found closed gates. The resurrected gathering at dawn in Quetzalcoatl Plaza, and at the shops throughout the realms, to buy provisions before the tourists came flooding in, found their favorite shops closed. The disheartened tourists turned from the lot; an army of security personnel flooded into the Kingdom through the employee gates. Vans the mascot rat's signature aqua raced through the boulevards, men leaping from their holds. They herded the scared dead with tasers into the vans and drove them to the gates.

The Dead Kingdom

Guards stood under the marble arch with the decree: *Find Your Dream*. The dead formed queues along Main Street, U.S.A. They stood anxiously at the windows of the candy stores and on an escarpment of blue roses at the base of the alp. White tulips formed the smile of the rat king.

Billy and Clare struck west through the bowels of rides. Billy knew the locations of the surveillance cameras, the secret exits of the attractions.

They waded under the cellophane willows of Alabama Swamp-oree and the banjoing bears, into the dark hamlet of Swift's Voyage, piled treasure (painted casino coins) scintillating in caves.

"Will security kill you?"

"Perhaps," Billy said.

The work lights of the cavern came on.

Shouts through a wall—security men in the next tunnel.

Billy moved decisively along a canal.

Footsteps followed through the roaring of the Caribbean typhoon.

He pressed into a door in the bedizened rock of Solomon's Mines. A steep climb. Veins of calcium carbonate laced the cement.

A few tiring minutes. Clare's shirt ballooned. He turned to an opening in a cavern in the mountain. It looked on the entrance.

Personnel raised their tasers at the signal of a corporate officer. Through bullhorns they commanded the dead to move out through the entrance.

The lines grew longer as vans, full of children who'd tried to hide in Huck Finn's Stone Maze, dumped their captures. The dead advanced reluctantly. Security zapped them into trot.

A piercing yell came from the head of the line. The march halted as concerned resurrected broke away to put a dead woman and her crushed child on the brick incline.

A group of security men looked on uneasily.

Billy laughed.

The security men shouted them on.

Through the mouth of this cavern, Clare saw dead at the front of the lines pressed against a transparent wall between them and the outer huts.

Security tased with indiscrimination, plowing into the crowd. A band of Civil War infantry, Yankee and Rebel, fought back as a lone samurai disarmed them of their tasers with fluid jiu-jitsu.

Gunfire echoed through the candy shops. The crowd broke to the alcoves, revealing three bodies in Main Street. Shrieking dead squeezed flat against the chocolate displays. Snipers knelt along the parapets of the soda-fountain and shot cripples limping toward the arch of Taffy Town.

The corporate officer, with trembling fist, held off the fire.

The three bodies in the avenue—a nun, a haggard clown, and a Chinese miner—slowly rose. Amazed, they massaged their wounds. The cripples rose.

The samurai drew his wakizashi with refinement as rifle fire exploded. The corporate officer ran in the direction of the port-cullis of the Castle, its drawbridge rising, Apache warriors working the winch. They rained arrows from the sentry into his tan face.

The samurai ran forward, prosecting guards, while the Civil War infantry, with whoops of glee (Lee on his charger dashed elegantly ahead of them, saber out), beat ten security men down with their guns.

The emboldened dead erupted on their persecutors. They

flooded the kingdoms. They waved their portraits above their heads.

A pistol hung in front of Clare.

Its hefty metal stored the power he'd fed into nights of portraiture. The meager summation of his ambition in its quick steel. The Kid smiled softly at him.

"They lost the Kingdom the day they opened it," he said. "And, the day they hired you."

Far below was Old New Orleans. Artists huddled as avengers surged in. The dead kicked in the windows of the Glass Slipper hut. They shattered the valuables of glass, upturned candy and carts of hats and climbed the wrought-iron balconies, waved bonnets and panamas at the air. Immortals poured over the barricade. Thorn, vanishing under the flutes and horns of lashing minstrels, looked unimpressed. Billy pulled Clare into the final cave.

He found twelve men calmly staring. Air coursed over Christmas smiles concealed behind trumpets that they blew in benediction.

Their flared wings glimmered and careened, anchored to cables. They smiled at a celestial symphony they alone heard.

The imposing figure behind them, erect against a dark Pacific, was another thing: a commandant facing in disgust from his field marshals.

White nylon wisps whipped on his arms. His hind claws penetrated the concrete. From a portal came the grind of conveyors.

"Aim that equalizer the way we come. He won't bother you. I got the maintenance stair."

Clare circled the spine with his pistol aimed at the mane.

He had to see it, that red stare.

The Kid hissed. Clare planted in front of the prognathum, held a quartz cube embedded in the rock.

He savored the eyes.

Taxidermed—dead—it meekly examined the rails with pond scum windows onto a soul of animatron lever. This aberration had died before it could be born. Unlifted as the concrete the cords of its spine fed into, as the electric stream pumping its rust bones. He recalled his terror seeing its eyes from his toboggan. The echoing recorded scream. Just another mannequin in this museum of intricate faces.

The fiberglass angel eyes widened. The trumpets lifted on the wind in warning.

Here, Clare swore, in this armored keep of the Kingdom, he would draw the remainder dead and indebt them. He would take Nada on the fissured ice and desecrate her share of cement. They would crown her in a rotunda of steel and silence, and they would make love in the beds of crystal, and on an easel throne in the vista of the statue the sun would rise, the fiberglass saints blessing his reign.

A bobsled nosed onto the scene: the contact with the circuit woke the malarial glow. The eyes above his burned carmine. They stared incredulously at the little pistol.

Billy was firing. The percussion woke Clare, return shots coming from the maintenance stair. The toboggan rushed and banged down the tunnel as the monster hugged him.

He pushed, and grasped at angel cable, cement, spray.

———

The Dead Kingdom

The light hurt his eyes.

His eyelids were lead, his mind an unworded knot. He moved instinctively to put out the light. Around his legs he felt whispers of children at a game.

He came through the resistance of shoulders, and cautiously to the hole. He put his eye into the sliver falling onto the stone. It poured into his spine and his mind cleared.

A Ferris wheel stood on a gold river. Silver pythons sped over scaffolding. Trysts moved along the asphalt, lingering between huts, in clothing of hundreds of eras, that he knew: their illumined heads floated through the relaxation, sureness of aristocrats in an elysium. A great mountain stood at back of them with the grandiose flare of a lax king. An arch wrought with jewel broke the neon into splinter; against it a man in a sombrero leaned smoking.

Clare pried. With the fever of memory he entered the Kingdom.

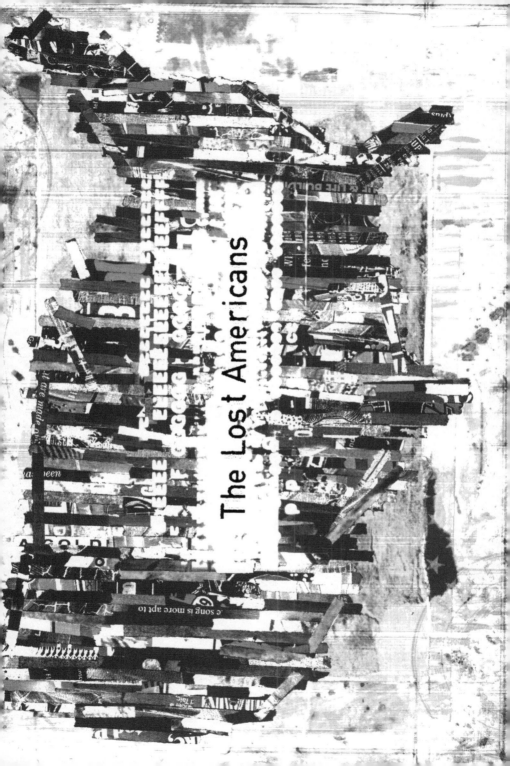

The Lost Americans

At Box Canyon a woman moved out of the ravine's shadow; my father cried out.

She looked up and recognized us. She sprinted the ravine, searching the stone with her hands. Unable to find holds, she stood in the silt, ankles cutting braided water, stare unmistakable through cataracts. Others on the platform squeezed by me to look into the ravine.

Shadows moved around my mother, jostled her, feet plashing through the stream as they emerged.

The maelstrom of shadows swept on some inertia around the bend into shadow, once more. Cries went through the crowd along the lookout. She vanished with the horde, screaming. A few lingering figures caressed the walls below, massaged the stone to coax it into stairs. Behind me the cascade hammered, drowning the excited whispers that rippled through the crowd as more pushed down from the lot. Cold water stung my eyes. The bolts trembled with weight. "Goddamn people," my father said, and shuddered through. We came into the rare Colorado sun, "—too many of us."

LOST AMERICANS

Familiar faces fought past me down the steps, late. They had stopped like us with their loved ones here, and now examined the gorge with lonely, loving eyes, an insane hope to see their dead. We saw them at Hoover Dam, climbing the Tejon in swaybacked RVs laden for the trip. At gas stations we passed them at midnight. Their eyes, in reunion scenarios, flared in our lights.

These Americans would travel with undying optimism across this continent piercing each corner with their headlights, until they met with their dead.

Creosote's Reconquista of us was ended. Coast desert burst from concrete. Haciendas shot from the vanishing lowland condos and the suburban light that reached into the deserts wilted toward the luminous city towers. Homes melted around their owners and the dispossessed moved west to downtown. The adobes of a hacienda grandeur long vanished watched this procession like dying conquistadors. Their arrogant stares washed in turn into manzanita and quartz, retinal impressions of flame, as other time elements entered our world. Present and past left us, tectonic plates shaken and shifting, and in the streams of invisible time our remembered dead spewed like pumice.

As we climbed the Tejon that final night the city shone like magma in the rearview. The new land was dark and inhospitable. Nothing could be seen past the cones of the lamps.

"Will we come home?" I asked him later. We sped down from Box Canyon and the Colorado towns we had vacationed at years ago. The low mesas floated by in the moonlight. The dim console irradiated his irises in salmon arcs while he smoothly held the wheel.

"Don't know, Chuck." Looking at me, irked, he made his voice softer. "I hope so. But we can't expect much."

"Why?"

He gave me the look he gave me when I spoke like a child younger than I was.

I tried. "Because she's dead."

"Bingo," he said. A minute later, he regretted it. He reached to squeeze my knee. "Either way," he said, "we'll take a longer trip. Do the plains, see the Great Lakes and Mammoth Cave. See where I grew up."

"If it's there," I said.

"If it's there," he said, not hearing, thinking of her, lost work, the beauty of the desert night.

We scanned the moraines of Navajoland. Cars passed us.

She had come to him. At night in the mirror when he cleaned his teeth.

In her gown, to my room, sliding through like she had with her shadow touching me.

"He knows where to find us," she told me.

"Where?"

"He knows."

She brushed my hair back with her palm, dry and slight as a dead leaf. I wondered why she couldn't touch me with her pre-treatment skin, radiant, olive ivory.

"So many people's memories are in this house and this city. Coming here is like walking through a storm, hands beating me back. It'll get harder. Go into the desert." She looked toward the sienna corona of a lamp above the neighbors' roof. "Get where there are no memories."

I woke with the dawn covering my room in a blue ash. My father's unshaven face hung in the door.

Through the upheaval the owners of the company where he worked greeted him with less intimacy every morning. Their locus moved into the past as his pushed through time: they saw him as a green employee and his fealty deepened. They halved his salary twice.

The only constant realities were shared by families and tight-knit condominium communities. Facts fluxed the further you moved from those who breathed your air and heard the same sirens in the night.

One morning he walked into an office that did not know him. The next we put what we valued into the El Camino. We pulled into the avenue, and the house watched us with the unforgiving glaze of a child left to die. We crawled in traffic, its hateful eaves and windows already translucent as lost ideas.

The ridge: spines of lava lifting altostratus slab to the still stars. (I remember now, so many years later, clearly how the moon in the cloud burned the façade of ice; silhouettes ran the viaduct over the pillars, the children of the gods in the stars.)

My dad, anxious, tuned the Citizens' Band radio.

The voices of forlorn truckers broke in and out, talking across the air, their simple conversations sustained by hope that in hearing each other they would touch their own lives. The conversations of the CB staved off the ghosts.

They traveled the interstates. These truckers knew, but couldn't say, that this signal let them touch each other only. The cities behind them come undone; their families passed into adjacent valleys of time. The homes they returned to would not be theirs, the families they sought not there. Without other recourse, money to pay rent, they kissed their offspring and set out into the green evening into the known routes. But the southwestern sky was an unrecognizable sea.

At midnight we came alongside Chaco Road. The archaic boulevard rose white from the desert into the mesas no horse could scale, its byways branching over friable plateaus, ending in talus basins. Anasazi walked it, their shadows slow along the road they had cleared thousands of years ago, that had reappeared now from millennia in a glistening wound.

The adobe hovels on the heights of the mesas peered into our windshield. Anasazi crowded at their stone rim, watching the trucks on the interstate and their own slow dead.

We wound through canyons. At sun-up, we came to Canyon de Chelly. The cliff dwelling was lit orange by the dawn, and the river ran high through willows beneath the ruins.

He stood four hours in the cold under the rustling trees. The adobe ruins stared back in vindictive skulls across the air.

He whispered, getting in the truck, "Where then?"

A caravan of recreation vehicles lumbered like pachyderms around a cliff. The parking lot filled and the chatter of tourists covered the sound of water over stone.

The Citizens' Band fell quiet. He stopped the El Camino to photograph me against crimson recessions and the nameless monuments that rose from the desert. He tried to keep up the appearance of a trip.

The El Camino roared though the dark morning hours over the Great Divide. My father's stare held us to our course, his detailed memory of these routes pinning them under the wheels.

Coming awake I watched the moon rising over volcanic cones to the east. "Tombstone?"

"No," he said. "Too many tourists. You know she hated people."

I remembered her passing her favorite swap meet on holidays, and any movie on opening. She wanted silence. She read her novels on the divan by the window with me under her arm, while my father attacked his half-living cars. She wanted vacant desert.

Cancer did not change that. She asked for us. At the end she moaned, "Chuck, *Chuck*—" and when I came, not say what she wanted, not to burden, and stared into me with fever. At times, she stared quietly out at the strangely warm winter.

We came to Sticks Caverns inevitably—all the roads would have led us to that hole. Copper rainwater formed halos around the diner built into the mountain. The tour man stood at the counter and looked out the smeared window.

Alfalfa fields cut far into the red soil. A cinderblock liquor store, a pawn shop and rest stop were the town.

"Tour," my dad said.

"Thirty."

"Slow."

"Slow year."

He took our money. He followed us through the door to the mine.

Our aluminum gondola skimmed the canal. Colorful niches slid overhead. We glided below Titan's Crib, with its gold flows of calcite and carbonate, and Samson's Column, tilted from the undulating ceiling. With its diffuse shadows and purples the cave was the inside of an agatized cloud. The river smeared the luminous eyes and mouths of the grottoes into sardonic smiles. Passages wound away from the river as the tour man pushed the gondola through the water.

"Anyone down here?"

"No," my father said, and freed his arm from my grip.

The tour man, walking the gondola: "This is the safest you could be." My father shot him a look. "With all goddamn shades up there, you won't find one here." He spat watery mucus into the canal. "A few stragglers in the beginning, of course. One, two kids, an old crone, drowned here before they sealed the vents."

We glided in silence.

"Did they get out?"

"They ain't here." His small wet eyes shone under a passing bulb.

The gondola tocked against a dam. A rusted chain hung over the water pouring down it, guarding a dark beyond.

"To our right, the Tunnel of Titan . . . " The man indicated a portal opening onto pink recessions like a giant's clean and frozen colon.

"Heads a mile south, and straight down. No one's ever gone that whole tunnel." His russet mustache, oiled, shone, warm baleen. He stared at me and rolled the oar in his palms. He lit a Camel and looked back along the meandering liquid fires on the river.

My father stared into the void past the dam.

He was remembering. Meticulously, he tracked labyrinths of memory.

He found her on the sick bed. She was eaten under the mechanical fan, the hue of the January behind the blinds; lying in the backyard, with her magazine, the sun melting on vital olive thigh. My father raced to find the final version.

The guide's voice was hard. "Oh," he said. "No, damn, way."

Headlights cut through the cave.

The tour man jabbed the dam, vehement. "One goddamn infestation—" He stepped across the gondola.

My father checked him into the river. The guide slipped silently into the shivering metal colors.

Behind clenched eyes, he thought of her, pulling at her.

I remembered her coming home from the hospital, shaky, hat over face. She smiled when she saw me, making her way on his arm.

Across the dark a figure came, drawn by the incantatory important conversations he recited in a whisper. The tour man, trembling and snorting, struggled onto the bank. He stroked his mustache and thin hair and sat up against the limestone.

She was at the dam. My father opened his eyes to her drowsy, filled grin.

He steadied her and the black water coursed through her legs and she climbed onto the rocking vessel. Her gild ate the purple grimaces across the hull. The guide roved her bright chest with his eyes. We extended the pole to him. He yanked the boat.

"Ma'am," he said, and climbed in.

In the El Camino she put her face to my neck.

"We'll eat in the town," he said. "We'll make the Mojave tonight."

"We'll sleep in the dunes," she said. The light filtered into the windshield onto her tan. "Look for Cassiopeia."

Her hand was strong and hot. A waitress and the drying gondolier watched us pull onto the highway. I forgot them, silent into the steady road.

Waterman

RANDOLPH RAN ALONG THE PIER, PAST ME. IN THE WATER BELOW, A lone rider struggled to get outside through the churning current. Tireless, the rider ducked whitewater and sucked through troughs as towers of emerald shot from the pier.

A wall of water burst through the railing and into Randolph, who could not tolerate the lone stranger riding his swells. Crouched, he clutched the planks against the powerful detonation of the water on the walk; it tore his shortboard from him. The pale fiberglass fins snagged in the handrails. The board dangled over riptide pythons agonizing through the pylons. Raising the board, he shielded himself from the next volley, dove into the sky.

I felt Randolph paddling over swells, his conditioned mind roving, radar pinging emerald nadirs for momentum and rise. His powerful ventricles strove between his hashed lungs like molten lava within a volcanic thorax. He strode over the glass. On a crest the rider shot through the crusted legs, the watching children screaming.

Rondo and Charl surveyed the scene from the shade of Beach

Tower Three. I shimmied down a piling onto the berm. Rondo's poncho had been dampened by the morning mist; its wool hood cowled him like a wise monk. Charl, moaning and holding his chest, swayed while he watched the sea.

Charl's girl, Becky, leaned against a leg of Beach Tower Three, studying my face. "Will you save him, Wes?" she said, her voice soft, her tiny eyes arctic ice. "Will you save your idol when his moment comes? Will you cry? Will you dive into those waves, bad boy?"

Her girls, perched along the crosspieces of the shuttered tower, shrieked. Their staccato laughter crossed my skin like fine steel spiders. Their nylon windbreakers slapped silver through the shadows. "You'll have your chance to be a waterman."

"*Look!*" Charl shouted.

Randolph and the rider paddled for the same peak.

To tell who was who wasn't easy. The wave surged beyond the tide: buoys sucked into its dark face and its green shoulders stood over the pier.

"Someday," Randolph always told me those still mornings when his vision of his life and its conditions touched, "I'll show you."

His trim elegance, the line he carved in the six a.m. quartz, drew the other eyes that floated in the darkness. They rooted feet in the water to slow their boards to watch him. Leathered, meth-wan, they floated along the wave shoulder, faces buoys, pacified eyes watching his genius quads cut the face. They bobbed, and he sprayed the grimaces.

"Go out," Carly told me, her breath white. She was armored in his ponchos. "He'll teach you. You'll be great, too."

I smiled every time she said this but she would already be staring at him, drifting among the silhouettes.

Carly shifted feet now in the sand, which was getting warm, watching the wave from the berm, her blonde hair fire. The sun drilled through the gauze to light the sea serpentine. The reverse winds had started to pock the water.

The dueling men climbed the peak, swiveled, pushed heels into the green. Froth blessed them, showered from its crown.

Rondo groaning. The girls watching quiet.

Charl shouted: *"No . . . !"*

The wave devoured the men and boomed. Its foam hungered toward the pier. It hollowed. Whitewater broke on the cement; a castle rose.

Charl pointed to the cycle of water moving northward and away from us. The riders shot from it, slaloming white lines from boards into its hole.

"Nah. I don't think so," I heard Charl say. "You can't get out. They're underwater still; they're *gone!*" A holy man with a private wire to the Divine (he knew what we couldn't), Rondo smiled into wind.

Carly semaphored her love. Slowly, her arms lowered to her sides.

Randolph was the wave. Without friction he wove its wind-chipped wall, and, in a clean and mechanical unison, turned with the rider to the pier.

Carly feinted toward the pillars, the wet barnacles. "No, please, Randolph . . . " She reached to keep him from their sieve. From the roiling vertical phantasm a maw emerged, slid over the pier, ate walk and cement barrels, outlook. A fishing ledge.

I ran, they flew. The wave jacked from shallows to darken the sun. Sand drank my shoes; I tripped down the berm.

I came into the shadow of the pier. In light, Randolph's bedding shone amid pylon. They straightened into the columns. A mist of whitewater along the planking and through the pillars, over an army of ghostly arms. Randolph's eyes, pure serious, looked into me. The lone rider cut south, out into the sun. Randolph was staring and through me, through the cement ribcage of this passage, saw his home. Sought by phantom, his slight figure cut south. I hit chainlink and strained to follow, lost him to light.

A House on the Mountain

I WAITED IN THE EXECUTIVE SUITE, STARING THROUGH THE GLASS down the nave of the mall. A delicate plaster of Paris Santa perched on the peak of Christmas Mountain, rising into yuletide light. Through the caverns and snowy ravines red steam engines rolled, their dioded cabooses flashing advertisements. Santa Claus looked down, lascivious drunk archangel at the gates of heaven, numbed with the sins of the latest souls.

The mall was a war zone. Once peaceful playgrounds of cement mammals were littered with Food Court refuse. The orca showed signs of abuse, his smooth face carved with pen graffiti, his lips streaked with pink like a deranged streetwalker. The concrete trash barrels overflowed, onyx tiles smeared with sandwich paper. Bodies crowded into the bare stores, and the screams of tired children echoed through the great hall of the cathedral like the howls of suffering eunuchs.

Violence and mayhem had come to fill the mall as the destruction of the southland strip malls forced more people to shop this mecca. Resources thinning, Christmas Mountain was plundered, low-perching elves stolen, two of the trains circling the lower foothill arroyos torn out. Security put up a cordon around the mountain and posted guards permanently below Santa Claus.

It started four months before, when the first strip malls began vanishing into the night.

King Corp management did not hide their disappointment with my performance. With each new destruction—the meek strip malls of plaster and steel wrenched so brutally from the earth their gas lines combusted, leaving craters of melted gravel—another of the Number One Inland Property Owner's revenue streams was cut, along with one of my tenuous strings to my job. I was King's lead mall investigator. Before the attacks I had dealt with graffiti rings and massage parlor scandal. The destructions were above my pay grade.

The assistant investigators, seeing a chance to overtake me, tried for "rational" explanations at the weekly meetings with the King Committee. A cabal of Silicon princes, with tech billions to burn, leveled commercial centers as commentary on consumerism, they said. With "high-tech instruments" they'd left the plantigrade prints as diversions.

With the destruction of the 300th strip mall a month ago, the last of management's patience evaporated and the row of blanched faces asked my opinion for what seemed the last time.

I'd gotten desperate. I scoured historical archives, found a possible key: an account of an assault on the Ciega Hacienda in the period of the conquistadors. On Día de los Muertos, 1799, during the raucous festival of music and light, a surprise attack razed the Ciegas' presidio. (The Spaniards charged local Indians and subsequently raided and enslaved them.) Other unexplained destructions—always of structures of light—riddled the pioneer era. The incidents tapered with the suburban boom after the Second World War—a retreat from an invincible force?

I had hoped this information would lend credibility to the strange eye-witness accounts.

The first reported sighting came late on the piedmont, a month into the siege. At midnight on Diablo Boulevard a "white monster" was seen galloping from a burning nightclub into the foothills.

A week after, what drunken witnesses described as an "albino buffalo" leapt onto I-60 from the smoldering debris of a stadium-church. A hundred thousand church lights twinkled as the cross listed over the ten-thousand-car lot.

The culprit grew bold: the damage reached the coast. I had my first believing moment in the beach town of San Anton, a quaint, rich enclave fifty miles from the piedmont.

Columns of a mini-mall colonnade had been shredded like piñata, their inner hollows of pine and aluminum torn open to the air. Enraged at finding no candy, the perpetrator mashed the mosaic walk and roof, punctured the plate glass of the Checks-4-Less cleanly as the cellophane of a dollhouse window. The cars of 24-hour masseuses lay crushed under the decal pole, in a nougat of melted lightbox.

The psychotic, but methodical, quality of the violation of this mall suggested darker forces than idle princes of tech. Prints led cleanly through the debris to an aqueduct whose channel ran to Bald Mountain, shrouded in smog.

Warm air had come up the coast in the night. Beachgoers

crowded the cordon, and through the din I heard winter swells relentlessly bash the sand as I leaned against an intact pillar, a trace of new fear moving up my skin.

Sightings of a nondescript white creature kept coming in.

"Whatever it is," said the latest junior executive risen through fallen CEOs. "You will kill it where it sleeps."

Insomniac leers of the executive committee converged on me, keen to believe anything that might save them money. I promised I wouldn't disappoint. They dismissed me.

I searched a department store for a gift to appease my wife, who would not be happy about my orders to hunt the creature through the mountains. Below morgue-like fluorescence, the children's section was ransacked, toy trains and pool blasters, hula-hoops and stuffed koalas strewn on the carpet. The ravaging of the women's section had been more strategic, only a few cable-knit sweaters on the shelves, tangled around themselves, the red and green heads of medusas. Pedicure tubs, neck pillows, ointment bassinets and all-in-one television remotes towered by the escalator rail as children darted through stripped clothing racks. Deep in the bowels of the mall a woman screamed, at missing a last pined-for item, or in ecstasy at the Daily Sale.

Tired, hypnotized by the Noël lighting and looping music, I found myself outside the festooned arch of the Grand Entrance Hall. The mountain blasted cold gales through the aisles of cars, warning salvos. Enraged customers shouldered out. The wind whipped trash from the asphalt into their legs. I had not bought anything.

A House on the Mountain

The night before setting out, we ate a quiet dinner beside the fire. Below our entertainment room, the inland valley twinkled to the sea, which we couldn't see, the low night smog lit internally as though with its own chemical glow. To indicate he knew (I felt, somehow, "it" was "he") we were coming, our adversary remained in his stronghold.

"You don't belong up there," Betty said.

"If it doesn't stop at strip malls?"

"Fewer outlets? It'll destroy anything in its way."

Embers blasted the fireplace tiles. She took my knee in her hands. "Please."

"We need my job."

She dropped her eyes, moved her manicured hands into her lap.

My work paid for this house, this view, our respectable two-bedroom in the foothills, in the mid-strata of smog where the air was lighter and easier to breathe. The job paid for our panoramic vista of millions below us. It paid for the comfort of their dim lights.

I could fall any moment. Any of the people below would eagerly replace me, take my house, my view. (My wife.) The American dream was not cheap, but steep. To avoid falling you climbed, fighting the cause of those higher than you, hoping to take their rock ledge.

"We'll live in an apartment," she said. "I'll teach aerobics, again."

"When I come back," I said, kissed her. "I'll buy you a castle on top of this mountain. We'll live so high, we'll see the ocean above the smog."

With a skeptical nod, her private shell congealing over her, she moved to the bedroom. I knew she lay awake. I sat in the living room through the late hours looking over the city. Since trying to have a child and failing, she had grown more distant, and neurotic. She didn't sleep. She ate little or not at all, then binged on supermarket cake, fish sticks. She pried with her compulsions into the mechanical guts of the universe to break the cog in our intercourse loose.

We hunted him.

Mercenaries, down-at-heel Special Forces retirees, were recruited to protect us. The ski patrolmen and park rangers led us over the high trails of the Gabriel wilderness. We explored every known peak. The ski patrolmen didn't believe in, or didn't care enough to believe in, the beast. Indolent surfers self-exiled to the mountains to ski the holiday snowfall, they couldn't have cared less if a destroyer lived in their range. If anything, they sympathized with it, an outcast like themselves.

One morning, after a snowstorm, I saw their jawlines clench, necks hold, the thighs of chained beasts in rut, while they looked softly at the supple slopes receding into the sun.

I had never been this high. The naked light burned my skin, which flaked away. This gave me a dark and sleek face. Nauseously I thought of my home, low in the pollution. The bitter air at my yard's elevation, the aura of the city basin from my windows, lingered in my throat, ashen.

A dark cirque fanned evenly from the foothills below Bald Mountain into the night, statistically ominous, cinching Mount Rencer Plaza Mall.

Did our adversary truly believe he could kill our light? Already the first strip malls erased were rebuilt with higher-wattage commercial complexes.

A House on the Mountain

Diode towers with advertisements for Tex-Mex and designer shoes, bath accouterment and Brazilian waxes rose from the coast twice as fast as our enemy could eliminate them. Sleepless, I imagined myself descending through ravines, cool manzanita and silently staring coyotes, into the stomach of empire, exposure guaranteed, to wage war with an invincible nightmare.

A scout found a path worn along a cliff. The mercenaries moved ahead, sweeping sights down the trail.

We entered a cavern. The rancid smell bit into our sinuses— fetid wool and meat. There were tunnels through the peak, with mouths opening onto vistas of the basin. Cautiously, we moved under the cave formations to the northern opening, and stood above hundreds of miles of desert. Ninety feet below sun-whitened bones blended into scree.

I watched the glow of sunset race before the shadow of the mountain. The capillary illumination of Tehachapi branched from a thick vein, the transcontinental highway, feeding to Inyo and Death Valley, a road I had never driven but suddenly wished I had; wished I was on it, driving now to the Sierra.

One of the rangers tapped me at midnight. I assumed a seat near the southwestern opening, my back to rock.

A few hours before dawn a shadow crossed my sleep. I saw Betty in her wedding dress, shining harder and colder than ivory, on the brittle lawn of our new home. The lawn incised into the tor of Bald Mountain in a hideous scar, healed over and emitting her wintry light. It filled the barren desert basin with a pale effluvia like the murk of bad fluid tendriling down from her dress. She smiled at me, the slick tubers of porcelain from the hem penetrating deep into the dark stone to arouse me. They opened and mapped me, cutting in beams of warm water. The stone stirred.

A shadow approached my dream. Hot breath beating against my eyelids, it catalyzed the dark mask I wore into epoxide. I saw the condensation of the breath on my nose sealing an armor. I saw my dark face awake.

Cold and sweating, my heart pounded. I scanned the cave. The views of desert and sea burned clearly. The lights seemed to have warmed the quartz in the walls, veined the faces of the men with death. My hands probed my face, felt the cool tan the sun burned into me.

Through the following days, we found no trace of the beast.

Betty saw my fall coming. Without a word, the night I descended, she perused condominium rentals in the desert. Stoicism hid her disappointment, barren womb filling with desperate anger, and terror, at the thought of losing our home.

A door opened behind me in the corporate executive suite as I looked through the glass down the nave. I noticed a commotion at the foot of Christmas Mountain. The crowd swelled inward as three guards clubbed into a vortex. Screaming competed with the carol.

"It would be a nice view to have?" the CEO said. He was new.

Right below the office, the crowd moved languidly, nudging politely into the vendors, unaware of the distant violence.

I turned.

The man's wide face was a shrewd predator's, watching for the slightest hesitation. He must have found none. He extended his hand and I took it. His teeth flashed in the citron of the map of the coast basin on the wall. Tacks demarcated destruction sites.

When I didn't speak, he said: "If being a corporate assistant was the best you could do, would you die happy?

"I doubt you would," he said. "And this goddamn thing—it won't go happy until it gets its prize." His eyes held mine.

"The Plaza Mall."

"Exactly." Without offering a seat, he swiveled to indicate the panorama of shoppers. "Your monster can level a thousand strip malls and won't dent a percent of the business we do in a Noël Weekend." He pointed a glossy finger to the spots on the map panels. "Haunted, this thing moves closer to its phobia through stand-ins, look-alikes to the needed star, getting the nerve. It'll come."

"You want me here when he does."

"He?" He smirked. "That's why I kept you. I think you *know* him—though you couldn't get a peek at him in his own fucking bedroom. You know how he will come, through what backstreets. You'll greet him."

"He'll attack the brightest first."

The Botox mouth sleekened on cigar, smoke veiling his dilute eyes. "Then you'll give 'him' his present under the tree."

I paced the perimeter on Christmas night.

The head of Mall Security offered to send men with me. An inexplicable mulishness made me shrug them away, wander alone.

Snipers with elephant guns posted inside the Christmas

Atrium. In tree stands, ten snipers hung within the evergreen, sights aimed through the glass entry at the silhouettes of the mountains. Civilian-camoed mercenaries occupied every nook, reading fashion magazines and jewelry catalogues. Others took positions in the subterranean parking, in dumpsters at the back of the mall, along the roof. Mercenaries with submachine guns lay below foliage tarps on landscape islands on the avenue.

Consensus was the beast would come through the ground, exit the runoff channel on the west side of the Crimson Pavilion.

Motion-activated spotlights with their own generators had been concentrated in the shrubs along the ditch to illuminate the monster the instant he came out of the sewer.

After circling the building once, I patrolled the front. Mountain Avenue climbed gently into the foothills. The Grand Tannenbaum evergreen burned unfazed in the entrance.

A handful of day-after shoppers scavenged the empty mall. A fraction of the customers of the night prior, they were ten times as violent. Shouts broke out over last items. A middle-aged man snatched the bottle of a fadding perfume from a sixteen-year-old girl; three boys ripped the latest gaming console at exactopoint from a scared mother. Security prosecuted these crimes quickly, without the usual interest.

Looking at the mountains, I thought of the house that would be mine, our children loping over its green Bermuda in the air above the smog.

The beast appeared in front of me.

He came across the intersection, the traffic light washing his filthy white to mint.

His claws clinked as he moved onto the sidewalk toward an

embankment of ivy. I froze where I stood twenty feet away. The protective arc of the Tannenbaum felt a cosmos behind me. The beast sniffed the air above the ivy. The matted wool of his legs dangled cinderized ornaments of restaurants and tanning salon.

Tenderly, he lifted his paw—like a bear's but four times as large—and set it in the landscaping. He slid down the gentle embankment on his haunches, coming to rest in front of me.

My walkie-talkie snarled. The sound elicited a twitch of the black lips, which peeled from yellow incisors. He had the eyes of an albino rat, grossly amplified into traffic lights, infected.

I closed my eyes.

Sour odors twined my face. I looked. A giant pupil was inches from me. Its shotgun diameter ate the light off my skin. I saw the Tannenbaum, the flowing serpent of the freeway, in its lens.

Deeper in the eye the city shone, bright as traumatic memory, the serpent of the freeway flowing into his optic canal. I was an absence in this brittle light.

He snorted and ran past.

Before he did I saw the scabies burrowing condos into his pectoral majors. Stadiums of high schools, duplex apartments, scarred his abdomen colorfully. The inland avenues crossed his forearms in slender setts. The Plaza Mall nested his navel, protruding, ruby blood, and I saw a small me in the parking lot of a fungus fading into his legs.

He galloped toward the enormous tree in its reinforced glass.

Halfway across the parking lot the motion sensors felt him. Klieg lights dogged his body. Sirens blared and he dove through the Atrium, trampled guards, leaped through the trumpeting angels of the tree.

Section by section, the lights of the tree died. The Tannenbaum crashed down the great cathedral.

The beast eviscerated the mall. Booms of guns, wails of shoppers and mercenaries faded until only the freeway hissed softly in the dawn.

Corporate laid his body in the foothills of Christmas Mountain. Santa Claus peered down at the body skeptically.

One by one, residents of the county and cities, victims of his campaigns, paid respects. They took pictures with their children's heads poised between his yawning canines, mouth locked in a breathless roar toward the broken glass of the King suite.

They nooked infants in his de-liced armpits, confused toddlers standing with fists triumphant, conqueror stances wide on his scars.

From my living room, high on the mountain, I look into the light.

The window is two stories by forty feet: almost as large as the mall entrance. Smog blankets the city; but the light pierces me. It eats, weakens, the special armor of my face.

The ocean twinkles deep into the night, planed diamond.

Betty sleeps. My twin daughters share a room.

I no longer sleep.

With my bedroom windows taped with velvet, the coastal basin finds my eyes, shining from inside.

Someday, I say.

A House on the Mountain

At my back, the cold mystery of the mountain whispers. The loud
lights swarm and drown its message before it can be deciphered.
Someday, I mouth. Someday.
Someday I will descend, and save the night.

THIS MESSIAH'S EYES DIFFERED FROM THE USUAL. THEY UNSETTLED, calculated; they were alert. They knew what I would say before I said it. The discs of his pupils hung in the sunned face with an inert tranquility I had seen survive the street in serial killers and violent psychotics. The eyes of saints never stayed like that after living for years in flood outlets, their stares dulled when they came to the ward, opaque and lightless, like sanded glass.

I sat with the messiah in intake asking the standard questions, checking the boxes.

"History of depression, psychiatric disorder, suicide?

"Hospitalization, psychiatric or otherwise."

"This is a first for me; far as I know."

I looked at him, caught by the subtle timbre of his sarcasm—not sure it was sarcasm.

Yet, in other ways, our man was unimpressive for a Christ. An overgrown bowl haircut made him look like a giant, neglected toddler, his face long and sunburnt, but retaining some of the chub of a smooth childhood: the face of a homeless twenty-nine-year-old or pampered, middle-aged son of a Tycoon, it fit with the faces of the adult children passing through our ward on their journeys from abused childhoods into neglected old age. Faces still paved by dim innocence after being used relentlessly by the shits of this desert kingdom for pleasure and distraction, and preserved from cynicism by the dimness of their minds, unable to fully reason through the injustice. The ward overflowed with these faces, the same unshakeable naiveté and deviousness shining from a dozen eyes of every age. It was my job to help them survive: to pacify.

I hated the faces. I did love them, too, though less and less. I hated them for the helplessness they made me feel when the medications stopped working and they returned, always dimmer.

Through the window grating the Sierra impended like the snowy ruins of a onetime stronghold, smog veiling the slopes. My eyes cut to the caged wall clock: nine. It was the time Jess always woke. I imagined her eyes opening serene to a room she thought, still dreaming, her childhood bedroom, to a world and a life she liked. And I saw her face when she remembered me, the cellmate.

"The police think you're a danger to yourself, and maybe others," I said.

"Then I must be."

Again I locked his stare, trying to gauge him. The strange lucency shone, not hostilely, intelligently, nimbly, the engaged eyes of a playful wolf.

"Is there a chapel in this hospital?" he said.

"Interfaith. You'll gain access when you've made progress."

"Towards?"

"Stabilization."

"I'm not stable?"

I told him not.

"You'll tell me when I am?"

"Why I'm here," I said, checked the boxes without asking the questions (I knew the answers).

He was looking to the peaks, the light gilding his eyes.

"We'll have *plenty* of opportunity," I reassured, cheerful, on autopilot, thirteen years making this rote: talk to the robot, "to chat. Get some breakfast and rest. Your medication will be at the dispensary."

"Medication?" Dry amusement in his eyes.

"Lithium to bring your mood swings down. Lexapro to help with the depression. An MRI, just in case—"

"Stroke?"

"A precaution."

"Schizophrenia."

"One possibility."

"You haven't asked me about my delusions, or *if* I have mood swings."

"Do you?"

"Do you?"

Smiling, I shut the binder.

"You haven't asked if I'm a leader from God."

He watched me, impenetrably. I stared back from behind my enamel grin. Then he smiled. A tension circled my neck: mentally ill struggled futilely, lost in dark catacombs of the soul, trying to get to me, to help. They couldn't, because I was with him.

"What else do you want to know?"

"You?" he said.

"I know everything," I didn't say.

I did.

I escaped without talking to him. It wasn't until seven, driving across the coast, that I realized I hadn't. Twice I passed his room, a silhouette against the aqua, looking through the bars as his schizophrenic partner wheezed.

Days passed. The messiah refused his medication: it would weaken the magic.

He had been arrested at Ankerton Mall proselytizing from the Christmas ambo under the giant Santa clinging like a frightened ape to its Holiday Mountain.

For ten minutes before mall guards arrived, he worked "miracles" and shouted. The crowd took him for a Christmas entertainer. A trick pail hung from his arm. Children's toys, electronics, nylon clothing dissolved spontaneously. From the grease he pulled lizards and serpents, throwing them into the people.

"Am I stabilized?"

"Can't give you access until you at least show a desire to improve. View it as an incentive."

The messiah turned his look to the water-rot ceiling.

"I'll wait as long as I have to."

"Cooperate," I told him, smiling, "and you won't have to."

Every noon he stood on the caged patio with the stationary bikes, patients cycling around him to freedom. He raised his face to the cool wind. The new and old patients shuffled into the entrance office and out as I concocted serotonin-reuptake inhibitor, tranquilizer, and alkali metal combinations for their checked boxes. Occasionally a patient left, mind glued long enough to meet state requirements.

Surprisingly, he fell into the backdrop, without the need of most messiahs to insinuate into all of our shit.

I tried to describe him to Jess. I found it hard to. She never pressed me. She didn't care. As I looked into the cool living room air, searching for words, she slipped to chop basil for our Wednesday night pesto, predictable as the desert sunrise through our window. We liked order.

The condo stood on a ditch lined in eucalyptus. The red bodies of men knelt over the creek, washing their clothes and bathing. With increasing frequency they came to the rim of the long drive that wound through the buildings to appreciate the vacant duplexes with desperate eyes.

The only occupant besides us was a widow at the far end. Between us lay twenty homes, empty, protected by two security cameras and the moral restraint of the vagrants. They patiently waited in the ditch, for work, for their abiding faith to pay. Less patiently, we looked to their departure from our property, the filling of the duplexes with professionals.

In the dark, I saw their retinas, wish-coins glimmering toward our balcony digestifs.

A warm sphere surrounded Jess that I couldn't penetrate, not anymore. Slipping down for a snack, she would ask what the plan was for food, kiss me, disappear.

She had fallen and fallen, before marrying me. I caught her.

During my medical school years, she idly studied for the GRE for writing school, a PhD in "medias," linguistics. She decided it was below her. I urged her to pursue music; she waited. She evaded structured solution.

After I had brought her with me to the Golden State for residency, a prodigal prince come for his throne, she started clinging to me at night, as if I were a ledge keeping her from a slide. This was love, I know. I watched her sleep, a panther I had mesmerized.

She took her credential in music, and her mind quieted into the SoCal expanses, our clean, well-lit home.

We married the summer after the M.D. I thought of her eyes impassioned in the sifting red light from the plastic windows of the chapel, often.

Years. Somehow children, imminent and nauseously exciting, never came. Next summer, when you get the production bonus. You know. A life that makes sense, self-sculpted, without Darwinian urgency, slid us toward death. The loess seamed the windows and stained the house pink.

When we first came to this corner of the desert, we cuddled on our calf-leather couch and watched the rocket towers rise in the sun. She held me. She asked about my work.

Now, I woke in those hours we used to spend together from trances.

Once, while she drank upstairs and I stared out, half an hour left me.

I heard a shout. Two desert men crossed blades of piss into a drainpipe. Another stumbled through the swaying eucalyptus. He cackled and wagged a bottle of gin. He saw me in the window before I turned.

He saluted me.

The roommate's narcolepsy improved. A 30-year-old schizophrenic, the man awoke one dawn and ate well, laughed over a bowl of Jello listening to the cafeteria conversations. He refused medication.

A late-stager, his neurodegeneration could only be slowed. He needed the cerebral concrete of antipsychotics. Because episodes came unpredictably, shearing away layers of brain in hours. But his improvement without meds left me no leverage. Klegman and Masamelli released him.

I asked Christ why he still refused the meds.

He didn't answer.

"You think you saved Carson?" I said.

"From?" He watched me. He smirked.

I checked the box: *persistent paranoid delusion (s).*

I placed a request with the County. The bureaucrats would transfer him to a live-in, but I convinced them. Doctor Masamelli, a shark smelling blood, saw my interest. He eyed me as he offered help. He regretted the messiah wasn't his.

She taught her Community College extension classes the nights I was free. As if it was fate, I didn't change my schedule.

I lay motionless to not wake her.

I found her looking at me. The diesels of 101 purred through the wall.

Something in her look made me think of the Jesus, knowing and distant.

She leaned through the space, and kissed me.

A rocket slit the night.

She rolled to me asleep, threw her arm across me.

She left.

Patients gathered at his knees.

One by one, in an ordered manner defying belief (and concerning me for the influence it showed), they shared their *feelings*. Comments ranged from the hopelessly manic to complaints about the food, spoken in turn in the same polite clip, all become drones of the messiah.

The nurses reported to me with burning eyes. These sessions calmed the patients. Docilely, they queued to collect medications they told me.

"He's like some therapist," I heard Amelia, an overly religious RN with a martyr desire, tell the nurses. She had an addiction to chocolate, was a virgin (for Jesus (I'd found her blog)).

From the recreation room he watched them move to bed. Our eyes engaged, his coarse features innocently a mask.

I sent a nurse to put him to bed.

The boxes rose in the foyer.

I made a pilgrimage to the southland Malls the day she left. I wandered through ivy, fountains of marble and suspension bridges piped in neon connecting the cathedrals.

Inner balcony displays receded; their contoured relics glowed (ossuaries of magic kings). Onyx broke the sun. I drifted, a ghost among consumers, their crisp moves buzzing locusts. On inspired heels, they snicked into stores. The sun beat when I exited through a designer-jeans apse and wandered, looking for my car.

I got home in time to shower.

I saw her blonde-white hair burn like a knife as she tumbled past the slippery cocks she grasped at. The sun shone in late winter and the hordes of anemics splayed on the steps of our college. I sat by the iron Roman goddess, working the hexenes of a diagram for orgo. I studied, and prepared, secretly, for my launch into power. We dated for a month and slept together and she grew bored and slid into the swamp again. She severed me, enjoying her young power in that swarm of flesh—most of it destined for theater assistant managership, third-rate law school, trust-fund itineracy, politically driven sex work, communist puppet circus. Her poets didn't love her. She liked me, but now, a spectator at my own wedding 13 years ago, I saw her over the white and black shoulders of the wall of my in-laws (their faces wet with gratitude (they loved me. They saw in me her greatest win.)). In her veiled face I saw the start of the dissociation, inner life which would flourish within my love.

Wherever he moved, my patients followed him. Apparently he melted slippers and raised indigo tapeworms from the petrol in the exercise yard. I upped his antipsychotics. His speech was clear, with his casual and mellifluous directness, his eyes on mine the instant I came into the hall where he happened to be loitering.

He used his inside voice. He didn't preach. He kept to room curfew.

He answered the question about harming himself, or someone, right.

One question he continued to answer with honesty: "Are you God?"

"Son of." He sometimes blinked after I checked the box.

We made small progress in therapy.

Then one day he said, "How's Jess. Is she still playing her music?"

The detective I spoke to said internet, everyone's information is out there, somewhere. Said call him if the messiah intended violence.

"How," I said, the next day.

His eyes' blue tuned to insolence. I saw an undulating flame.

"You told me in a dream," he said.

I followed him down the hole; I was losing control. "What else did I dream to you?"

He smiled sweetly. "You drive a Honda Accord because it's the best deal through several price classes, and you want the staff to think you're frugal. You want to be seen as humble. Although you want the new Porsche. You said your cock curves rightwards, and it's always worried you."

I signed an order for electroconvulsion—I would jolt the liar, and in the blank post-ictus get the truth.

He slipped out of the facility that night.

"I just don't like you," she said when I tried to stop her. "I don't think I ever did. I don't like myself. I can say this."

My generator jammed as it cycled insults.

"I love you," I said.

"I know. I'm afraid. I'm sorry," she said.

Can a sociopath be tenderized? Gently warmed into a softer pathology? I spent my life grouting the chinks in other makeups. At most, I sealed the faces they turned to me, helped them turn the metallic head of a doll to the infinite eyes.

But for a sociopath, could the schism between the continents be bridged? Jess knew. She was the only one who knew—I wish she'd told me what she knew.

Christ walked at dusk the next day into the San Dominion Mall. He rushed through the nave, ragged and tan, knocked the vendor carts of New Age Religious tracts and massages over, customizable ornaments. He jumped onto the hut thatch, under which Santa Claus took children upon his red engorged knee, and ripped up model train tracks, kicked out the cotton stapled to the roof. Before he turned to the crowd, arms spanned, security guards poured from the department store, and he vanished through an emergency exit.

He spent the next days at the white rock cliffs a mile from my condo. He preached from a pulpit to the indigents on a wild stream. Two men who told the police about it—arrested for sleeping on the embankments of the Mall—said he took the rock trilobites in the stone in his hands and made them live.

The following twilight he visited the massive flea market in San Telmo. He stood on the Christmas choir stand, transmogrifying used surfboards into Triassic iguanas. He ripped the boards from a vendor, piled them in the parking lines. He raised his arms to the green night, by the same method he'd melted children's toys melted the boards to a fluorescent pool. The enormous iguanas rose like the dead from their shrouds and moved through the screaming consumers into the desert.

"Be better," he enjoined the crowd, "than oil. Make this world worthy of the miracle that oil walks, that oil talks and multiplies across the Earth. You will all pass to oil. You were brought from it into the dream. The Lord does not fear silence should your noise and light offend him."

When the police arrived, he was gone. He was seen walking barefoot with his lizards into the hot chaparral toward the blue hills.

Stories of the messiah's sermons found their way to us. Several patients a day cheeked, had to be restrained, injected, inspired by him.

Finally, two firsthand witnesses of his works involuntarily came to the ward. Not hard for me to see their minds were corroded by ecstasy and peyote fevers. They imagined the creatures risen from the oil, the restoration of life. I made them stable with lithium.

I felt him coming. The image of the messiah struggling across quartz and bayonet yuccas to me warmed me.

I needed to give him his life. I waited. Checked boxes, redeeming. It became easier.

The messiah was seen climbing an arroyo, and was not heard from again.

After we fired the one nurse left alone at the controls the day he left, the ward fell into its ancient rhythm. I received a warning from the HQC (Hospital Quality Cunts). Delusions, false hopes he'd given, bled from their eyes. They ventured through their minds by my side. We confronted.

We found peace.

On my balcony, through the years, past the ditch men, tranquil, as I sipped my digestif, I saw him, as I closed my eyes.

Salsipuedes

FIGUEROA DETOUR: HERE COMES THE OLD WOMAN CORNER, ITS notched rim. The sidewalk cuts down, with the right angle of lift you grind that granite five feet up, a falcon the rim of a steel mesa, and land the wall on her drive. Clancy looks back to me over his shoulder. I feel nothing in my bones.

Knees, gentle ninjas. My front Independent hits. Smack, and grind, I land truck to the stone, quarried by Chumash at the bores of Spanish guns, sometime later removed from a sanctuary to be inserted in this hedge retainer. Gladioli, white roses, bob past my knees like dazzled old crones. I push with my soul to keep the inertia over the friction from the stone. I feel my momentum slow.

I float over cement. I wonder where Sarah is, and Bethany. I wonder this as I fall because I always wonder this, images of soft throats and ass-cut jean squeezed into my brainstem like ammunition.

I hit hard. Wrist shrieks and board shoots into street. A truck tire boomerangs it into blue.

"I told you," the woman yells. Screen snaps. "I told *you*—

"Son?" she says, standing over me.

"I'm—Whatever," I say, not meeting her eye, recovered, in sprint drop the board under gilded Excelsior Titans and bank into sun.

Downhill onto Salsipuedes, to Castillo, cracks clicking in our soles, the cars on fire in the sun. The air sweet with wind raked through sage over the Riviera, pollen from ripe magnolias: the coastal climate in rut.

We glide, into commercial stucco villas, windows onto wine bistros, suits like our fathers with their figurine ninth wives, gilded in ambience. Past the lighthouse on Juan Rodrigo and estuary canals that wend from the zoo along the white beach. On the bridge we halt. Dark lips sensuously open the water to our saliva. The jetty's granite quarried in Roosevelt's lifetime breaks with waves like pale flames.

Women come. We envy the wind that nips their Coppertone.

"I need a cigarette. My god . . . "

"You have those Reds we found?"

"If I did," I said, "would I say I need one?"

Clancy eyes me with aggression. "No—"

We soar into the slow swerve of quadbikes heavy with Iowans. The bowls slide into view, the old ivy dunes cemented for our pleasure.

On the quarterpipe rim the crew sits. The pungent smoke of their bongs impregnates the air like matins. Christopher White, without a shirt, displays a turtle abdomen cut with gold under the red sun.

Becky and three girls encircle his Serpent Titans. Other SGHS crew stare vaguely. The female hair flares on emerald tubes coming through the pier. Silhouettes on the glass, relaxed amid barnacles.

Salsipuedes

Becky's eyes follow mine through the complex. Her attention is raised to a kingly palm when I stand at the bowl. White squints, passing me with alert eyes, along the boulevard.

His slits tickle me with familiar shame: my junior-high face gleaming from the cover of the real-estate brochure, set onto the violet Mission and billionaire villas, state-spelling bee champion.

Two years of torment and isolation the tithe for being a "tart little bitch," White said that day in La Raza Park, when he and his crew confronted me beneath lashing queen palms. Homeless residents of the topiary Narwhals watched as White pressed his treads into my jaw (while I bled), the sun glinting on his abdomen as he stared at the Riviera, Jupiter looking home.

"Gonna go?" Clancy whispers. Such timing, leaning into my ear as I slot tail to brink.

"Do you *think?*"

His sneer flies into the air.

Concave sheers under wheels, delivering me into bowl. I grind the concrete island rising from pools, an altar to unthinkable delights, Independents whistling, slender steel to steel. I connect, cool, loose shoulders, baggy soul gaping easy into the ocean.

The central altar rails are anointed with stale wax. In water walk I glide by Becky. White tightens. The shadow of his abdomen digs into his gold.

A superbus of Japanese visitors honks. The faces stare attentively from their air-conditioned ease. A skater grips pine in low orbit off the altar, returns to earth slamming in a squeal of styrene into concrete.

Moans emit from shale faces.

"*Shit!*" Clancy shouts.

I perch on the wall, panting.

"Nice," he concludes.

"Go," I say, a generosity filling my neck. I want him to know the pleasure of inflected cement.

He looks into his smooth suede shoes (the hard metric of soul), then out to sea. "Later." I wiggle a toe through one of my Titan holes.

On a rusted bench we watch the soaring. A twelve-year-old with Einstein hair and pink infectious eyes offers a cigarette.

White rises, moves to us. His golden calves churning when he squats, he examines the Riviera through the palms. The thousands of house windows glint and reflect, embroidered ornaments in the tapestry.

He caresses my wheels. Their center stripes of grit hiss on his palm. "Spitpowers?"

"Hard Jelly," I inform him gently.

He knew this. He looks back to the mansions.

"Can I?"

He is the part of the wind, instantly, that cuts your skin. My wheels touch down, his khakis whipping spinnakers; he glides and pushes tail: his arced spine kisses steel. He contorts himself back over the deck. He soars, holding ply, lands linearly, power sliding my cylindrical jellies in an act of degradation.

"*Shit*," Clancy says.

I say, "Whatever," watching.

His abuse of the altar is of a true king. Independent trucks ding the stone and in a miracle of angular scarring he cuts the rail with the wood.

He gives the board to me. "Good."

Salsipuedes

"Sure."

"This thing," White says, casually glancing over the whitecaps to the islands. Tendrils of gold sinew circle Becky's throat, spreading her pulsing thighs of ivory to his hazel stare. "Tonight. If you wanna come . . . "

Becky watches through smoke.

We climb the Riviera in Clancy's family sedan. In the night the city sparks.

The houses light above us, insects with phosphor, mandible porches, windows the chitin facets of their eyes. The tallest homes perch dominant on Camino Sur, jostling out the smaller homes for vista.

The elms hang to form a tunnel. A sign indicates La Puesta del Sol up a drive.

The ghosts of forgotten starlets roam its stucco and sand-stone corridors, its Andalusian chapel, to haunt Midwesterners and New Yorkers, the few producers and actors who flee sets to this aerie, as well as newly weds on honeymoon from less classic cities. I put my face to the glass and feel its cold adobe. The Puesta floodlit, green beams bathing its white from within bouquets of yucca.

"Ho," I say.

Clancy takes the sharp turns furiously.

Clancy shoots me his best look. "Can't keep a cheetah from speed."

"What." I pause for impact.

"Sit back," he says, "and put your trust in the Lord."

He swerves, zooming into the soft dimensions of wealth. Multi-million-dollar Tudors turn to us like sex predators startled out of dark prowl.

We turn on Camino Cielo. We ride the spine. The engine revving, my toes crave traction.

Clancy says, with a deep reverential feeling, something annoying. He leans forward and I see the bright castle.

And we are into the Iberian light.

A tile drive curves through obelisks to the Moorish towers. My fingers curl around absent truck climbing the veranda.

We drift. Music from the vestibule, coming the length of the castle, is permanently far while with the flow we pass through geodesics. Wall and hallway fountains spurt into pools.

We enter an entertainment room the size of a modest community church, film screen covering one wall and dance videogame pistoning the stoned limbs of girls in tight bikinis, beer plashing from cups as they squeal. Colorful computer-generated ravers show them how to move. When their moves lock, stars spill from the walls of the room.

Girls look at us coolly. Inflamed stares of men track us.

Clancy moves mesmerized through the people, mouth open.

Chris White and Becky lift from a sofa, on an elevation in this tile court. Rings sail from White's mouth across the air. SGHS crew sprawl at their feet. Becky's ice eyes brush me on the way to someone else. Bodies push Clancy and me, deltoids telling me to get to a wall.

"Go say hi," Clancy is saying, shouldering me to the sofa.

Salsipuedes

"*You* go," I say, shove him, and turn to a comforting noise drifting in.

A half-pipe rises outside on the patio. Through the crystal, bodies melted by bevel. It hypnotizes, and vasodilates warm blood into my groin. I glance a last time at them before stepping out, and they look at me with expectation, seeming to command me.

"Skate?" White says.

"No." Crescendo, showers of stars. "I FORGOT IT . . . "

He flicks a finger. He looks off. He looks at me. "VERT?"

He nods at my nod, smiles, the nacre of his angelic mouth reassuring all who believe.

(Two girls from the ninth-grade squeal as his brother Eric bastes their tits with cognac.)

He nods at Becky, who watches me.

A sprawled crew member between my knees and her bare feet stares with pique into my eyes. I catch it, hesitate; as though to encourage me, he darts his glazed irritation toward the joint in her hand.

She grabs my collar and tilts: I suck smoke out of the velvet passage of her throat. White moves his hand somewhere over her, she releases.

Clancy catches me.

I try not to cough; my lungs burn. Bolts of white fire slam in my spine. Clancy grips me, searching my eyes for Becky and Chris White as I watch them above looking for new pleasures.

I am outside by the half-pipe.

Lanky figures follow the curves. They fall and rise on the vert. The stadium lamps flood over me: here, the feel from the hostility inside the castle washes from me.

Time moves imperceptibly and Clancy is gone to find his own niche in this kingdom. The timbre coming from inside the castle changes: Chris White stands in the door. His torso shines, cuirass of a great argonaut, his socks and Titans glacial and luminous. He takes up his skate, moves past me, inviting me with his cryptic eyes to join him.

I am on top of the pipe, an unfamiliar skate in my hand. Chris White stands beside me, reassuring still with his stern belief in me, which he shows with a smile. My skin sings in the cold wind.

Past the floodlights I discern the mountains, a row of courtiers in pale hauberks over whom the moon is a sad face, softly illuminating this tournament—someone I once cared for now lost to kings and grace.

I see Clancy down there. Two unwanted ninth-grade girls who through some third-party haggling made it in flank him. This pariah trio holds close together, dreaming of splitting their cocoons of worn flannel into my grandeur.

The inflamed SGHS Crew boys scream. Their skates rattle, and—they scream for me.

Clancy and his girls will never see the world from this high, not knowing steel. Control. The girls adore me. Tight shorts and stale shirts clamp cruelly residual fat. I want them to be touched and winnowed thin into svelte elegance, but I have to fly!

Chris might be irked. I slot my board; he nods.

We fall; we fall into glory.

The ground rushes. A gelid fist moves up my throat to meet it.

Salsipuedes

Toes, tendons, seize like terrorists. I see the stars, float toward them with the selection of a soul.

Big earth wants. Tugs. Calves and thighs, trained for curb, hold.

The vert might be the surface of a dimension. The grip in my feet dissipating, sensation from a severed face.

An angel above me, look: Chris, body in silver fire, connects with the rim. He sees me crumple. His face darkens with recognition.

My dick catches his nose. Khaki whispers on eyes. The curve gives me to the other vert, where we collide; we fall together.

The firmament presses on me. The horrified stars conceal themselves behind thin tatters.

I rest.

"Is he *dead?*"

Blood seeps from his eye. Becky, pale, kneels by his body.

The serpents on his Titans seem to slither away into his legs.

He moves his head voluntarily. I breathe. On a dozen arms, his torso rises.

A spike-lipped SGHS kid asks Chris, watching me, to say something.

Chris touches his brow, says uncertainly, "Sure."

"What are you looking at?" he says to me.

"You fucked," says someone.

"You dropped in on him . . . "

"There was intent."

I stand. "I swear—"

A girl. "You did."

The crouching ring is now on its feet.

"Well, bitch." Eyes imprimatur scarlet of decree, White says, "We thought you were good."

I don't move my stare from those hemorrhaged seals. My sentence lies behind them. Clancy backs into his girls.

The wind rinses my hair with my mother's insistence.

One of the ninth-grade girls: "*Jason!*"

An SGHS veteran, older and with a parmesan tint of hepatitis and prison tattoo, in a metal gleam rushes into the ring.

I take up the board. Chris screams. Crowds pour into the patio area.

Stradivarius of bowed rail carries me. Assault fire shudders, the cracks of tiles, in my tibias. Behind me the crew rolling, but my leg has thrust, and his Spitpowers take me into the hills.

The moon watches me through the tunnel, bright as it emerges, a forsaken friend who has awaited the chance to forgive; the cold air from the ridge washes my skin as the men fade.